M000306214

The Tarot Mysteries by Bevan Atkinson

The Empress Card
The High Priestess Card
The Magician Card
The Fool Card

THE EMPEROR CARD

A Tarot Mystery

by

Bevan Atkinson

Acknowledgements

I am indebted to my Gentle Readers, Nancey Brackett and Judi Cooper Martin, who with infinite patience encourage me to keep going.

A double thanks with extra sparkles goes to Lyn Adelstein, for her invaluable assistance with website and book design, and to her and John Kremer for their marketing savvy.

The staff at Book Passage in San Francisco and Corte Madera could not be improved upon; they foster and promote new authors, and their Mystery Writers Conference is a great event.

Hannah Mikles at the Boulevard Café, Chris Hess, and David Young provided much-needed editorial oversight, as did the awesome Afrikahn Jahmal Dayvs.

Mike McGowan, Alexandria Marcotte and Bryan Alexander of California Gold Mining, Inc., were expert guides into the gold mining realm. Walt Costa did the same for police procedure.

I also want to thank my Too Much Fun Club cohorts, Laurie Sain and Tracy Blackwood, for we are far-flung fun-loving friends forever.

To the English teachers at Winchester-Thurston School who, in spite of my peevishness and insolence, inspired and encouraged me as they did so many others:

Mrs. Beard
Miss Millar
Mrs. Luckie
Mrs. Beebe
Mrs. Widgery
Dr. Harshbarger
and a special thanks to an angel
Mrs. Ann Peterson

"I felt very still and empty, the way the eye of a tornado must feel, moving dully along in the middle of the surrounding hullabaloo."
　　　—Sylvia Plath, *The Bell Jar*

"Our real discoveries come from chaos, from going to the place that looks wrong and stupid and foolish."
　　　—Chuck Palahniuk, *Invisible Monsters*

"Whoever survives a test, whatever it may be, must tell the story."
　　　—Elie Wiesel

≈1≈

I don't know about you, but I'm not accustomed
to coming home on an airless sultry day, letting
the two excited, capering dogs out into the side-
yard dog run, going upstairs and peeling off my
clinging downtown clothes, taking a tepid shower
to wash off the stickiness, clipping the tags off of
and sliding into a newly purchased gauzy sun-
dress, pouring a lovely tall glass of iced mint tea,
letting the still-excited dogs back into the kitchen
and giving them a treat, carrying the plastic glass
of iced tea through the curtained French doors
and out to the deck to see if anything resembling
a cool breeze from the always cold Pacific Ocean a
hundred yards away would please blow the edge
off weather my friend Chris Sears refers to as "hot
as fried hell," only to discover a dead body in my
back yard.

Finding a bloody, supine corpse in my fenced Japanese garden is, to me anyway if not to you, a considerable shock. I dropped the iced tea, and ice cubes and tea splashed onto my flip-flopped feet. I broke out in goose bumps and a case of the shivers, no cool breeze required. I mostly just stood there gawping mindlessly for a good long time.

I gawped at the man's long body, at the edge of the man's face, his features pressed into the carefully raked sand. I registered the body as that of a gray-haired Caucasian. What skin I could see, except for his cheek, was tanned. For a moment I took in the shape of his sprawled left hand.

I forced myself to expand my focus to his partly untucked and shabby white oxford-cloth dress shirt and faded navy slacks. A leather belt cinched the fabric into pleats at his waist. This man had lost a lot of weight without buying new clothing to fit his smaller circumference.

I could see the outline of a sleeveless undershirt beneath the collared oxford cloth, the tan skin on his torso silhouetted against the white of the undershirt. He didn't have a golfer's tan; he spent time outside without a shirt on.

One down-at-heel black lace-up leather shoe had come off and was resting sideways next to his left foot. A black sock was pulled mostly off, the baggy toe flopping empty on the sand. The exposed heel showed roughened white cracks.

Rusty brown dried blood had soaked the back of his shirt. A long knife blade glinted next to a tuft of tall grass a few feet away from the corpse.

Blowflies buzzed and dropped into a trail of swarming ants. A momentary breeze bearing an indescribably awful smell woke me up from my gawping.

I took a deep breath through my mouth, let it out slowly, and backed through the French doors, heedless of tracking cold wet tea onto the floor of the darkened house.

4 The Emperor Card ה

≈2≈

Before calling the cops, I called Thorne.

"Steer clear for the duration," I said. My voice shook when I said the words.

"No," he said. "I'm on the way."

"You are not," I said. "Of course not. Don't even consider coming here until everything has settled down. We'll meet up later to talk about what to do."

Thorne is so far off the grid that his existence is offensive to the bureaucrats who like to keep track of all available humans; for instance, the IRS, the Census Bureau, the Department of Motor Vehicles, and any and all police officers.

"I don't care," he said. "Better me than you."

"No. I can handle this."

I started to sob.

"Babe," Thorne said, and waited. I pulled myself together.

"Something very strange is happening here," I said. And then I told him what he knew anyway, because I needed to talk. Just talk and talk.

"You and I both know that when anyone is murdered on your property they look at you first. Meaning me. I have an alibi, and I have identification. You have no ID and they will arrest you, and then they'll want to keep you forever because you have nothing to prove who you are, or why they should let you out of their sight. Please, Thorne. Unless you murdered the man out there in the yard, you should stay away."

He was quiet, which is what he generally is. For a moment I wondered whether he was actually responsible for the dead man. I ruled that out when I realized that of course Thorne was capable of homicide, but he could not have been responsible for this one, because if Thorne had killed this man the corpse would never be found; it certainly would not be dumped in my garden for me to come home to after a long muggy day full of errands and shopping.

"Buy a burner phone and give the number to Nora," he said, referring to my sister, who with her husband and multicultural array of children lives nearby, in a far ritzier San Francisco neighborhood than I can afford—although affording real estate of any kind in San Francisco is out of the question for anyone who didn't start the process somewhere back when the T. Rex, not the mortgage broker, was the alpha predator.

"Your world is going to devolve into preposterous chaos," Thorne said.

He attended an haute-WASP prep school back East and went on to Princeton and Harvard Business School before becoming a big bad wolf of a bodyguard. Every so often words like "devolve" and "preposterous" slip out.

"I know. I'll deal with it. And maybe we can meet up later at East-West," I said.

The East-West Café is our go-to choice for off-site refreshment. Since I never cook, nor should anyone want me to, available off-site refreshment is a major priority.

"Yes," he said. And then, "I'm here. Always," except then he was gone.

I called 9-1-1 and the dispatcher told me to go stand outside the house and wait for the police to arrive, and to stay on the phone until they did.

"I'm going to lock up the pets first," I said, whistling for the reluctant dogs and carrying the pair of dozing black cats up into the third-floor bedroom that serves as an office, where I shut the door on all of them.

Yes, two dogs and two cats constitute a lot of pets, and one of the dogs—Hawk, the black Great Dane/Mastiff mix—counts as three or four or a dozen dogs at once. But I'm a grown-up now and I can have as many pets as I want to while I'm eating ice cream for dinner. Nevertheless, herding them all, especially Hawk, out of the way of armed minions of the law seemed like a prudent thing to do if the soon-to-seem-endless parade of law enforcement personnel were to enter and exit unthreatened by such an imposing pooch.

Outside on the front steps, I sat myself down with the phone to my ear and waited for the preposterous chaos to devolve into high gear.

Which it did.

≈3≈

It turns out the police show up extremely promptly when you alert them to the presence of a recently murdered person. I had only just plunked
myself down onto the front steps when a siren
howled around the Geary Street corner and
sagged down to silence at the curb.

"They're here," I said to the dispatcher as I
thought of poltergeists and hung up.

A pair of patrolmen followed me through the
house to the deck. Once they saw the body they
split up. One officer stayed on the deck talking
into his shoulder walkie-talkie; the other took me
back into the house and told me to sit while they
summoned the required troops.

I sat in a chair by the front window, and as
more police showed up one stayed with me and
one was posted down at the front door. Crime

scene technicians and medical examiners and assistant district attorneys and deputy coroners blocked the street and came inside.

It was still hot, and I yearned for a replacement iced tea, but I sat, dry-throated and uncomfortably warm, letting the activity swirl in and out of the house.

An unmarked sedan parked and out stepped someone I knew, and into the house he came. Up I stood to greet Walt Giapetta, pulling my dress away from where it clung to the backs of my thighs.

"Xana, are you okay?" Walt asked me, taking my hand in both of his. Walt is a sort of friend of mine, or at least he was on the way to becoming one.

Maybe not, after this.

He was wearing a creased dark brown lightweight suit over a starched cotton tab collar shirt and a red tie with a matching dark brown check. He'd unbuttoned his collar and loosened the tie; given the day's exceptional heat I could hardly blame him. He studied me carefully out of muddy brown eyes. His thick graying hair, combed into gelled rows, swept straight back off a low, oliveskinned forehead.

"I am not particularly okay," I said, looking up at him. "But I know everyone has a job to do."

"I may not get to keep the case because you and I know each other, but for now I'm the one assigned. The bureau is busy enough that it may stay with me. Whoever handles it, you can be sure the detectives will do everything necessary."

He turned, remembering. "This is my partner, Detective DeLaRosa."

He gestured toward a woman with skin the color of old ivory who looked at me the way I've seen birds of prey study rodents. Gold stud earrings glinted from under short dark wavy hair. Her pantsuit was navy linen, crushed into a riot of wrinkles at the end of the humid day.

"Whatever you need, Walt." I caught myself. "Sorry. I'll call you Detective."

"I need to ask you some questions."

He pulled a folded handkerchief from his pocket and swabbed his glistening forehead.

"Sure," I said. "Would you like some iced tea? Or some ice water? I want some anyway."

I wondered if I was a suspect. I didn't ask him. Of course I was a suspect.

"Give me a minute, please," he said. He went back downstairs to talk to the officer at the front door to the house. I stood with Detective DeLaRosa and kept quiet. I sat down again.

"Detective?" Walt said, back at the top of the stairs, waving his partner over to where he stood.

"Sit tight for another few minutes, please?" he called back to me as the two of them went past me, pulling open the French door curtains and stepping out to the deck. I nodded at his back.

With the curtains open, sunlight flooded the room. I sat and thought about iced tea. My designated patrol officer stood silently by the picture window, ankles shoulder-width apart, hands clasped in front.

"Where can we talk, out of the way of the tech team?" Walt asked as he came inside.

"You tell me. I didn't notice any signs that something happened inside the house, but I can't guarantee that."

"We're already in here, so let's start here for now. But at some point we're going to let the techs have the house." When I looked a question at him, he explained, "We have to establish a wide perimeter at first. We can always narrow it down later, but we have to be sure we haven't missed anything by assuming a smaller crime scene than is actually the case."

Through the kitchen window I saw an officer stringing yellow tape around trees in Sutro Park, next door to my property. Outside the front window a crowd had accumulated across the street.

"Let's sit at the table, shall we?" he said, pointing toward the dining area.

"Sure," I said, allowing Walt to take charge. I followed him across the living room to the dining table, next to the archway into the kitchen.

"Before we sit down, give me one second to check in with the crew again," he said, and headed outside.

I waited. Detective DeLaRosa sat and waited with me. We didn't talk. Walt returned after a few minutes, a clipboard holding an inch-thick sheaf of papers in his hand. He squinted at the hot glare of afternoon sunlight through the French doors and pulled the curtains closed.

"So far there's no evidence the crime scene is anywhere inside your house, but we're just going to talk for a few minutes here, and then I'll need you to come downtown."

"Downtown? Why?"

"Your house is a crime scene, Xana. You won't be able to get back in here until we release it. And I need to take some time with you, to go over what's happened."

"But my dogs?"

"Do you have somewhere they can stay, in case you're away for some hours? Or we can move them to a shelter."

I thought for a second, first about jail, and then about allowing the dogs to be hauled off to a cold, concrete pet prison for even a minute, as if Hawk would go willingly. I told Walt my sister in Sea Cliff could probably pick up the dogs. Why not, after all, since what difference could two more living creatures make in a house with fifteen children?

I was not thinking in a sisterly fashion right then. Nora's kids love Hawk and Kinsey, but adding more to her daily workload is not a sisterly act, no matter how much the nieces and nephews adore my pets.

"Sure. We'll figure that out when we get to it," Walt said. He took off his jacket and, hanging it carefully across the back of his chair, sat and turned to me. Detective DeLaRosa reached across the table and he handed her the clipboard. She clicked a mechanical pencil to push the lead out and started filling in blanks on the first page. If I looked at Walt I could only see her peripherally. I looked at Walt and ignored her.

"I'm going to record this conversation, to make sure we both know what we've said."

He took out a little recorder and held it up for me to see. I nodded.

He tested the device, then pushed a button and recited the date and time and who we both were and what we were going to talk about. As he managed the recorder I noticed fine black hairs, glossy in the light slanting in from the kitchen, on the back of his fingers.

Across the back yard fence I saw a woman with blue paper booties over her shoes stepping slowly back and forth within the yellow-taped-off area of the park, looking down at the ground as she went.

"What is your full name, please?" Walt said.

"My full name is Rosalind Alexandra Bard. But I go by my second name. By my nickname, I mean."

"And your nickname is?"

"Xana," I said, pronouncing it "Ex-Anna" the way my infant sister Nora had first done many years ago, doing her baby best to manage "Alex-andra" and failing.

"All right. First, what can you tell me about what happened?"

"Nothing."

I lifted up my hands in a shrug and shook my head. I could feel my eyes begin to sting and I felt the heat of color in my cheeks. I cleared my throat and swallowed to keep the emotion at bay.

"So let's talk about what you do know. Tell me about your day."

I inhaled a deep breath and let it out slowly, collecting myself. Walt listened, Detective DeLaRosa jotted, and I answered question after question, most of them repeated at least once.

What time did I leave the house this morning? How did I get downtown? What time did I arrive at the dentist's office? What time did I leave? Where did I go immediately after that? How did I get there? How long was I there? On and on, until I was finally back home, calling the police with cold tea drying on my feet.

"Did you touch the body?"

"Oh God no. No no no. I stayed up on the deck. I was really thrown for a minute, you know? I just stood there. Then I ran inside and called 9-1-1."

"I see. Do you know the deceased?"

"No."

That stopped the questioning for a minute while Walt thought things over. He looked at Detective DeLaRosa, but I have no idea what they communicated to each other in that look.

I was trying, and occasionally failing, to only answer the questions I was asked. I have a friend, an assistant district attorney, and over the years I have paid attention to her case descriptions, during which she snickers unkindly at the foolhardiness of testifying witnesses who elaborate and embellish instead of answering yes-no questions with "yes" or "no."

Having paid attention to Lizette the prosecutor, I worked hard on telling Detective Giapetta the truth, nothing but the truth, and nothing more than the truth. I wanted to corral the truth, because as I'd sat waiting while the chaos devolved I'd remembered something, and the memory nibbled at my conscience.

Walt's phone buzzed. He stopped the recorder and answered. He pulled out his phone, looked up sharply at me, studied his phone some more, held it to his ear and spoke.

"Text the photo, would you? And bring me the wallet?"

Walt stood and went down to the French door, pulling on latex gloves as he walked. A tech handed him a battered-looking brown leather wallet. Walt unfolded it to look at something, then handed it back. Walt's phone buzzed again, announcing a text's arrival.

And then he was back at the table, pulling off his gloves, moving his fingers over the phone's screen, and finally clicking the recorder back on.

"Ms. Bard, I need to ask you again, do you

know the deceased?"

"I do not," I said, looking another question at Walt. Why was he asking me again? But he *was* asking me again, so I hedged. "At least I didn't recognize him. I couldn't see his face."

"Who is Josiah Wayfield Bard?" Walt said, turning his phone to me, showing me a driver's license photo.

The overheated day shrank down into a black spot and my ears rang. I don't believe I was breathing.

My world had just devolved beyond preposterous chaos into straight-up hard-core insanity.

18 The Emperor Card ה

≈4≈

I felt Walt's hand on my arm, holding me upright in the chair. In the center of the black spot I saw my hand on the dining table. I flashed back to the shape of the dead man's hand, at his fingertips that, like mine, bent upward at the last knuckle.

"Water," Walt said, pulling my chair back and lowering me gently in half so my head was on my knees. I heard Detective DeLaRosa's chair scrape back and then the click of cupboards opening and shutting. A tap opened and water ran.

"Keep your head down until you feel better, and then drink some water," he said.

The world started to expand from the black dot and then I was back in my dining room, by the ocean, in San Francisco, with two detectives hovering, one holding out a glass.

I sat up slowly, looked at my hands, and said nothing.

Walt took the glass from his partner, holding the rim to my lips. I took a sip.

"Who is he, Xana?"

I took the glass from Walt and looked at my hand holding it, took another sip, wiped the wetness from the glass with the hem of my dress, and set the glass on the polished mahogany tabletop.

"Josiah Wayfield Bard is my father's name. And that photo looks like my father, but thinner. My Dad was always a big, husky guy. But that man outside can't be my father." I looked up at Walt. "My father died many years ago."

Detective DeLaRosa, back in her chair, had flipped over some pages and was taking notes again. She looked up, and then at Walt.

"Let's set that aside for now," he said. "When was the last time you saw your father?"

"A very long time ago."

I thought back, counting the years, matching the passage of time to events Before-the-Divorce, After-the-Divorce, Before-Dad-Died, After-Dad-Died.

"Nine years," I said. "My parents divorced and then he died. He disappeared before the death. Two or three years before."

I was startled that I couldn't remember exactly when my father's funeral had been, or when I had last seen him. Apparently Walt was not buying it either, narrowing his eyes and looking his next question at me.

I forgot about answering yes and no.

"My father was a drunk," I said, sighing the words, slumping against the hard wooden chair back, gripping the edge of the table as I spoke. "He wouldn't, or couldn't, sober up and stay sober. My mother told him he had to go, and he went. One day she told us he had been killed in a car crash."

"Us?"

"My brothers and sisters and me."

He wanted their names, addresses and contact information, and I told him my sister Nora, the potential dog harborer, was the one in Sea Cliff. My three other siblings lived in other cities, and their addresses and phone numbers were in my address book and phone, the address book being in the office upstairs and the phone being in my purse on the front hall table.

He paused and pinched his lips together into a fishy mouth while he pondered what to ask next.

"All right, we'll get those from you in a few minutes. When your father left the family, did he go peaceably?"

"Yes."

"Any contact after that?"

"He called me from time to time, for a few months anyway, wanting to see me. I was his oldest daughter, and he and I were close while I was growing up. So I agreed to see him once or twice, but he was always drunk and kept trying to justify the drinking by blaming it on my mother. God knows Mater would drive anyone to self-destructive behavior in a wide variety of flavors, but Dad was the one doing the drinking and I decided he bore sole responsibility for that.

"I told him point-blank that he had to stop if he wanted to continue our relationship. When he didn't stop I unlisted my phone number. He came by the house a few times, but when I saw him outside the door I could tell he was drunk so I never answered the doorbell. He stopped coming around after a while. And then he died, and at his funeral I was a mess, so I got a lot of therapy and it helped me, and here I am."

"Was the relationship ever violent?"

Walt left unspecified by and against whom any violence was perpetrated. I looked back up into the cop's alert dark eyes.

"No, Detective. He was just a sad man who drank too much. He loved me and my siblings and probably even my mother, and we all loved him, and then he behaved in such a way that we felt we had to put him out of our lives. And then he died. Or at least I was told by my mother that he had died in a car crash. There was a funeral, and someone's ashes—I thought they were my father's—were scattered at sea."

"Can you explain how the victim in your yard has the same name as your father?"

"No. But if that man is indeed my father, then his appearance is very different from the man I remember. And if he is indeed my father, I now have to have a conversation with my mother and my siblings that is likely to be monumentally awful, because if it turns out my mother lied about his death my relationship with her may never recover. If she's kept the truth about Dad a secret, it's possible I've now lost my father twice and my mother as well, not to mention there's going to be a second funeral for Dad, which in my opinion is too many."

My voice was shaking, and it sounded too loud to me, and my eyes were full of tears. I was angry with myself because I heard self-pity, if not downright whining, in my words. I jammed the tears off my cheeks with the heels of my hands and tilted my head back to sniff them down my throat so that tear snot wouldn't slide out of my nostrils. I hauled my self-absorption back under control and tried to smile.

"I've had a lot of therapy, and I thought I was over needing it anymore, but I see a major psychological tune-up looming."

Walt saw a box of tissues in the kitchen, fetched them, pulled two out with a whuff whuff sound, and handed them to me. Through the thin fabric of my tie-dyed sleeveless float I felt the tweedy chair upholstery prickling my legs. I remembered that under the flimsy fabric I was wearing only underpants. I crossed my arms over my breasts to prevent nipple awareness.

Walt waited until I had wiped myself dry and made eye contact with him again.

"Where was Mr. Bard during all these years?"

"I have no idea."

I had managed to recalibrate the tone of my voice to something closer to its usual alto.

"Where was he from originally?"

"Here. The City."

"Does he have other family here, besides you and your sister?"

"He had a married sister in Palo Alto. Aunt Jeanne. But she died of cancer before he did. Before we thought he did. His parents are both dead, of alcoholism, and Jeanne's husband, Uncle George, died not long after Jeanne did. I don't know of any other relatives."

"Who were his friends back then?"

I remembered the New Year's Day parties my parents used to host, with multiple televisions set up around the house tuned to the Bowl games. Women in cocktail dresses and men in suit and tie drank too much and talked too loudly. Caterers in black pants and white shirts offered silver trays full of crab puffs and smoked salmon canapés, neatly furled cocktail napkins in their other hand.

"He was an investment banker. I believe they have contacts, not actual friends. At least I'm not aware of anyone showing up or even calling after he lost his job."

"Had he ever been married before? Or did he remarry after he left your family?"

"Not that I know of."

"Do you know how Mr. Bard came to be in

your back yard today?"

"No."

Walt looked over at Detective DeLaRosa, who nodded, and then back at me. I took a deep breath and let it out, gearing myself up to answer the rest of the detective's questions.

"When did you discover the deceased?"

"At about four-thirty."

"Let's go over your whereabouts again today, while you were out."

I told Walt again about my day: the mid-morning bus trip downtown to the dentist, the shopping foray to Ross, the lunch at Le Centrale, the afternoon appointment with my friend Maury the CPA, and the Uber ride across town to my house.

"When did you get home?"

"A little after four o'clock."

"So you were gone from ten this morning until around four-thirty this afternoon?"

"Yes, I've been out all day, since this morning. Except I got home at more like four-ten or four-fifteen. I let the dogs out, got into the shower for a minute, put on this dress, and poured a glass of iced tea before I went out to the deck at four-thirty or so."

"If you let the dogs out, why didn't you see the body then?"

"I let the dogs out from the kitchen. The kitchen stairs go straight to the side yard that's a fenced dog run. I can't see the garden from the kitchen door, and the dining room curtain was pulled across the French doors to keep out the sun."

Walt asked me more questions to pin down precisely what I'd done during the day and after I came home. I answered them.

"Xana, was Mr. Bard here when you left this morning?"

"No, he was not here. Or if he was I didn't see him. I have no idea how or when he got here."

"Do you know what happened to him?"

"I do not. I saw the knife lying in the sand and the blood on his shirt, but I didn't go down the steps to look at him."

"Do you know why he was here today?"

"No."

"You say it's been years since you thought your father had died. Can you be more specific about the last time you actually saw the victim?"

I looked up at the detective. The truth and nothing but the truth, I thought, and here we go, straight into preposterousness and chaos.

"I think it was last Friday, ten days ago, but I can't be positive."

Walt and Detective DeLaRosa sat up, still and focused, like setters alerting on a pheasant.

I shrugged and kept going.

"I'm just realizing there might be a connection between the man in my yard and the guy who was outside on the sidewalk one morning when I pulled the car out of the garage. If it was my Dad,

I didn't recognize him. The guy I saw was much thinner than my Dad and much older-looking. He had wild gray hair and a long scraggly beard. My Dad was always very careful about his grooming, but the man who approached my car looked homeless, you know? Like he hadn't bathed, and was sleeping rough. He called out something but I didn't really hear it. I think now that he might have said my name. Anyway, he tried to stop the car but I drove away as fast as I could. I was a little freaked out. He was gone when I came back later that afternoon. If it was the same man as the one in the garden, then that was the last time I saw him until I came home this afternoon. I didn't recognize him lying there in the yard. The clothing is the same, but cleaner, and the man outside has had a haircut and a shave."

"I don't see how you could not recognize your own father." Detective DeLaRosa spoke for the first time.

And now I knew I was a suspect, and when I answered her I could hear the protest in my voice.

"Prior to last week I hadn't seen my Dad in nine years. Sometime in August nine years ago. But now that you've told me the man's name, it could be it's the same person who called out to me last week before I drove away. But I did not then, and I do not now, recognize the person in the back garden, or the person who tried to stop my car, as my father."

Well, everything changed, as I had known it

would as soon as Walt showed me the ID photo. I
expected Walt to recite the Miranda warning now.
His deep-set eyes had gone flat and hard.

"Detective, I was out all day and I can prove it
with witnesses and receipts. The blood out there
has dried and the bugs have found him. I don't
know when he was killed but whenever it happened I was on the Muni or downtown or in an
Uber car. And I still don't believe it's my father."

But of course a part of me did; the part that
had registered and matched up our fingertip
shapes when I first saw the body.

A slender thirty-ish woman with short curly
red hair and a galaxy of freckles across her paper-
white skin came in the house and whispered in
Walt's ear. She was wearing a French blue polyester pantsuit and a white shiny knit collarless
blouse. I stared at the tight weave of the fabrics,
wondering at her opting, in this weather, to don
head-to-toe polyester. For her, washability out-
ranked comfort, I suppose.

Walt thanked her and she walked away.

"Who else lives in the building with you?"
Walt said. She had told him about the downstairs
apartment with men's clothes in the closet.

"I live on the second and third floors. I have a
tenant living in a ground-floor in-law apartment."

"What is the tenant's name?" said Detective
DeLaRosa, her pencil poised over the clipboard. I
hesitated, but then said and spelled Thorne's first
and last names. Nothing but the truth.

Now Detective Giapetta frowned at me. I had met Walt while he was working on a murder case in which the victim, Mona Raglan, had been Thorne's client. Thorne provides premium personal security services, which in everyday parlance means he's your big old bruiser of a bodyguard, hired by very rich people willing to pay him in cash. I had met the woman he was guarding because I read tarot cards, and she had asked for a reading.

After she was murdered and her husband had been shot as well, Thorne disappeared, the way he does when the real world is likely to impinge on his invisible existence, if a six-foot-eight, two-hundred-sixty-pound person can be considered invisible. The murderer confessed and Thorne was not a suspect, but Walt had never been able to question Thorne about Mona Raglan's murder, and he didn't like it that a material witness had eluded him.

I couldn't blame Walt, but there's no way Thorne could accommodate, or come out unscathed from, police questioning. Thorne converts the cash he is paid for the work he does into gold, actual coins and mini-ingots, and locks the gold up in a storage unit safe. He converts the gold back to cash as needed and pays for everything as he goes—no credit cards or ATM pin numbers involved.

He likes it that way, so that's the way it is. The cops would not like Thorne, his ID-free lifestyle, or his Scrooge McDuck money bin one bit.

The problem now was that, until this moment, Walt had not put Thorne and me together except as unrelated, coincidental witnesses to that previous murder. In my every-so-often lunches with Walt at Caffé Sport in North Beach I had never mentioned Thorne, nor had I let on that I had a tenant, nor had I announced a boyfriend. Thorne would prefer not to be the topic of other people's chats.

During the garlic-infused lunches I hadn't exactly flirted with Walt; he's married and off-limits. But I think Walt enjoyed the idea of having some one-on-one time with a younger woman who laughed at his jokes and was willing to listen to his same old stories.

I think I mostly enjoyed the idea of being enjoyed, and I wanted to learn more about what a detective does. His same old stories were new to me, so I encouraged the storytelling.

Walt was clearly wondering about the new fact of Thorne's co-residency with me. The situation was thoroughly questionable: a man who could be my father was dead in the yard and the current possible boyfriend was missing, having likewise gone missing after a previous murder.

When Walt spoke again his tone was carefully neutral.

"Where is your tenant now?"

I noticed the way Walt implied a set of quotation marks around the word "tenant."

"I don't know. He's had a client for the last couple of weeks. He generally sticks pretty close to the client for the duration. I didn't see his car when I got home, so he's likely on the job."

"Does your tenant know the victim?"

"I doubt it very much. Mr. Ardall has only been living downstairs for a short time."

"Do you know when your tenant is likely to be back?"

"I don't. His work takes him away from here, typically for weeks at a time."

"Do you have a phone number for him? Or do you know who his current client is?"

"I don't know who the client is. To get you his number I'd need to look at my phone," and I gestured toward my purse sitting on the entryway table.

Walt got up to go get it. I was silent while he was gone. Detective DeLaRosa was silent too, glaring relentlessly at me, the no doubt faithless and disloyal daughter who had probably committed patricide.

Walt handed my purse to me after looking inside it briefly. I suppose he wanted to be sure I didn't have a .357 Magnum in there. He probably missed my miniature Swiss Army knife, with the toothpick and mini-scissors attachments, and was unfamiliar with my uncanny ninja skills when deploying this little masterwork from Ibach, in the Canton of Schwyz.

I tapped at my phone and displayed Thorne's

number, for all the good it would do Walt to have it. I was certain that Thorne had turned off and thrown his old phone away as soon as he ended our earlier call.

Walt jotted the number down and then stared at me for a moment, letting the silence build. I looked at my long fingers with their short, nude-polished fingernails, at the tilted knuckles that were just like my father's.

"Anyone else been in your house today?" Walt finally asked.

"The dog walker would have come at around noon."

"Does he let the dogs out into the yard?"

"No. She just opens the front door and they come barreling down the stairs. Molly gets their leashes from a hook in the entryway and loads the dogs into her truck. She takes them with a lot of other dogs to Fort Funston or one of the other areas where they can charge around off-leash. When she gets back she lets them in, hangs up the leashes, and they have the run of the house."

He asked for and I gave him Molly's contact information. I heard Detective DeLaRosa's pencil writing it down.

"All right, Ms. Bard. I need to speak with you more about your day today, and about the victim, assuming it is Mr. Josiah Bard. And if it's in fact your father, we'll need to have you formally identify him. Let's make the arrangements for your dogs and then we'll go downtown."

I called Nora and asked if she could come over now and pick up the dogs. She heard something in my voice and said "Right away," without asking a lot of questions, bless her.

Ten minutes later, when she got as close as she could down the street and climbed out of her car, I walked the dogs to her through the cluster of squad cars and vans, handing the leashes over and telling the dogs to sit while I told her everything but the presumed identity of the dead man. I wasn't going to light all the fiery family torches until it was beyond doubt that my father had been resurrected, only to die again amid the gray-green grasses and round river rocks of my Japanese garden.

Back in my front hall, I felt semi-naked in the gauze dress. I asked Walt if I could change clothes before going downtown. He said yes, for which I was grateful, but stopped me before I could start upstairs to my room.

I stood and waited. After a few minutes Walt came back with a forty-something Latina, her hair flattened inside a net, white latex gloves on her hands.

"Chanel Martinez is a crime scene technician, and she's going to scrape your fingernails."

Walt was not asking me, he was telling me.

I held out my hands. Chanel took a sharp little tool and held a plastic bag under my nails to catch whatever came loose, which was not much.

"We're going to need your clothes," she said.

"Do you want this too?" I gestured at my dress.

"Everything," Walt said. "Chanel will go with you to collect it all."

I led her upstairs along the narrow path at the edge of the stairs that Walt pointed out. I pulled my damp slacks and blouse out of the hamper and dropped them onto the wide sheet of butcher paper the technician spread across the floor.

Chanel wanted the underwear I'd worn, so I retrieved the bra and panties from the hamper as well. I unhooked the sandals I'd been wearing while downtown from the shoe rack.

"If you were wearing those sandals, I need to take scrapings from your toenails," she said. I sat down on the bench at the foot of the bed and let her do that. She then asked for the dress and clean underpants I had on.

She told me I could change in the bathroom, so I grabbed a robe from the closet and went into the bathroom to swap out what I was wearing. I gave her everything and she tucked the garments into individual paper bags and went back downstairs.

I dragged on another pair of underpants, my cutoff jean shorts, a bra and a tank top. I laced up a pair of running shoes, without socks because in the sauna-like heat the thought of socks was repellent, but I couldn't imagine wearing sandals to jail. I pulled a cotton cardigan out of the closet because on the rare muggy days in the City you can always hope against hope for the cold fog to come rolling in.

I heard the inner voice that calls me "Child" say, "Take your cards."

I opened the sandalwood-lined rosewood box on my dresser and lifted out my silk-wrapped deck of tarot cards.

I opened the third bedroom door, confident the cats would stay huddled out of sight until the coast was finally clear of coroners.

Downstairs again, I poured out kibble and fresh water for the felines, picked up my purse, shoved cards and cardigan into it, and followed Detectives Giapetta and DeLaRosa out to their unmarked police sedan.

I was pretty sure I was going to jail. I was pretty sure I wouldn't like it.

≂**5**≂

A lot of stuff happened while I was down at the Hall of Justice at 850 Bryant Street. Mostly I was treated to the various aromas of despair: industrial beige paint, stale tuna salad, human sweat that smelled like chicken soup, and the occasional pong of piss-soaked concrete in the stairwells.

I'd been fingerprinted and then escorted to the fourth-floor squad room where the detectives worked. While I waited in Walt's cubicle for someone to ask me questions or take me somewhere to do something investigatory, I pulled out of my purse a Christopher Fowler mystery about the Peculiar Crimes Unit. I thought Bryant and May would have felt right at home with what was happening. I forced myself to focus on the lines on the pages instead of thinking ahead to a body cavity search and an orange jumpsuit.

Detective DeLaRosa returned at one point and told me that the coroner had taken fingerprints from the victim, and that someone—I suppose it was Walt or Detective DeLaRosa or a crime scene investigator—compared the prints to the various databases. A match came up because my father was an investment banker, and all bank employees are fingerprinted for the Feds.

After that Walt told me to put on my sweater because we were going downstairs to the chilly morgue. I slid in a bookmark, tucking the novel into my purse after obediently but slowly pulling on my sweater. I wasn't looking forward to the descent into corpse identification territory. I went anyway.

In a room smelling of carpet dust, decomposition, and throat-choking formaldehyde, I saw a monitor displaying an image of the person Walt said was the one found in my back yard. There, behind the ashy pallor of the slack skin on his lower face, and in spite of the closed eyelids over gray-blue eyes just like mine, lay a thinner, older version of my previously deceased father.

At least I was almost sure. I had goose bumps from the cold or from horror or both when I asked if the man had an anchor tattoo on his left bicep. They pulled down the sheet and redirected the camera for me, and I saw the tattoo and the words "U.S. Navy" across a twined rope.

So I was completely sure, as opposed to mostly sure.

I must have started to make noises, because Walt put his arm around my shoulder and turned me away from the screen, shushing me the way you soothe a hurt animal.

When I managed to suppress the moaning Walt asked me to confirm Josiah Wayfield Bard's identity. I did, and we went back upstairs where Walt sat me down, asked me if I would be all right for a few minutes, and left the detectives' room, saying he had to finish up with the coroner and designate me as next of kin when it came time to release the body.

I felt stomach-churning nostalgia and surging regret and recrimination. A buzzing undertone rang in my ears as I came to terms with the fact that I had failed to recognize my father last week. I agreed with Detective DeLaRosa: How could I not have known it was him? I stared at my Bard family fingers.

I looked around the office to see if anyone was paying attention to me. No one was. I pulled the tarot pack out of my purse and unfolded the scarves. I sifted through the cards, looking at the images, waiting for something to register, something that would help me grapple with what was happening. The Queen of Wands caught my attention and I stared at the card.

"What are those for?"

Detective DeLaRosa perched herself on the edge of Walt's desktop and eyed me with what seemed like a carefully composed non-expression.

"I'll put them away," I said, rewrapping the scarves, shoving the deck back into my purse.

"Don't tell me you're one of those woo-woo people, with the crystals and the candles."

"It's San Francisco. The Board of Supervisors passed an ordinance requiring every citizen to be into woo-woo or face fines higher than the ones you pay for parking in a handicap zone," I said, hoping to draw a smile from her.

She did not smile. "Do you take money for reading them?"

"No."

"Really? Isn't that all those things are good for? Cheating gullible old women out of their life savings?"

I felt my face heating up in a blush of annoyance. I knew better than to answer her, so I didn't. I gazed calmly into her dark glittery eyes and guessed that her mother was one of the gullible old women who'd been cheated by unscrupulous fortune tellers.

Walt walked up and, without shifting her eyes from me, she told him that my timeline for the day checked out, meaning my alibi.

"By the way, where do you work, that you could take the day off?" Detective DeLaRosa said.

"I'm self-employed."

I was ducking the question. I don't have, nor do I need to have, a day job. I've learned that saying "I don't have to work" annoys some folks. I could have recited a saga about a wrongful termination lawsuit and monster financial settlement, but saying I'm self-employed is a lot easier and usually stops the questioning cold. Not so with Ms. DeLaRosa. Probably why she's a detective.

"Doing what?" she said.

"Consulting."

Calling what I do, or rather don't do, "consulting" is the second line of defense, virtually guaranteed to stop people from prying. "There be dragons," at least for most people, who understand that "consulting" is likely to be a euphemism for "unemployed but unwilling to say so."

Not this detective in her crinkled linen. She was not to be deterred.

"Oh? What do you consult about?"

I went with the vaguest thing I could think of: "It's a kind of life coaching."

I'm sure "life coaching" is well defined somewhere, but I unaware of anybody who wants to know more about it whenever the topic arises.

The reality is I volunteer one day a week with a third-grade class, helping out with kids who need attention or help with English or a new set of colored pencils. The rest of the time I do what I please, and there is a great deal to be found in San Francisco and indeed the world at large to please me.

From time to time I also read tarot cards for people, and I felt the weight of the deck in the purse resting on my lap.

The upshot is that I don't typically announce

that I'm a litigious, unemployed tarot reader, unless I want people to clutch at their wallets and make swooping Theremin whining implying unexpected weirdness on my part, that or they mouth off about charlatans and gypsies. I think they think they're being funny or else justified, as Detective DeLaRosa seemed to feel.

Meanwhile, if they belong to a Bridge club or play Go Fish with their kids they're using tarot cards, so I wish people would calm down. Just chill, folks, and keep shooting the moon and slapping the jack.

Meanwhile, Detective DeLaRosa was not tolerating my evasions.

"What does a life coach do, exactly?"

A smile that looked very much like a "gotcha" grin spread across her mouth. Walt looked at her, a question in his expression. He hadn't asked me about my employment or lack thereof because we had discussed my status during our now-and-again lunches. But he wasn't going to stop his partner from asking. I imagine he wondered why she was bothering, since my alibi checked out.

"Fucking earthquake weather," a man said as he came into the office swiping a brown restroom paper towel across his forehead. I blessed him mentally for the interruption.

Long-time residents of San Francisco think that when the temperature and humidity soar the earth is going to tremble; both the 1906 and 1989 "Big Ones" took place in Singaporean heat and humidity. The theory is nonsensical. We adhere to it anyway. The implausibility of the theory aside, we prefer our weather the way it should be, the way it is just about every day of the year: cool and dry or cool and foggy.

I looked around, taking in the non-color of the cubicle dividers contrasted with the people standing around them. It struck me, the care with which the swing-shift detectives sported suits, ties, socks and shoes that allowed them to look professional but individual. Their ties added the only vivid color to the nondescript room.

"It's not going to cool down tonight," I said, shaking my head and fanning my face with my hand, treating Detective DeLaRosa's question as if it were mere small talk, as if changing the subject was perfectly okay to do.

Walt started talking again, and I ignored Ms. DeLaRosa's steady gaze communicating that both she and I knew I had not answered her question.

"Thank you for your cooperation, Xana," he said. "The inside of your house has been cleared, but the yard is still unreleased. So you can go home, but from the house itself to the backyard fences is off-limits, including the deck and the dog run. Anywhere that's taped off is going to remain restricted until we're sure we have all the evidence. Here's my card, and if you hear from your tenant please tell him to call me on that number, any time of the day or night."

I slid Walt's card into a side pocket of my

purse. Detective DeLaRosa was ready with her card as well, and in it went next to Walt's.

"I've called for an officer to drive you home," Walt said.

"That's very kind but, with your permission, I'd rather take a cab."

I figured the half-hour drive home would entail a shock-sprung vinyl-upholstered Crown Victoria or CV-clone that smelled of McDonald's, vomit, and fear.

"Cabs don't respond to this address very fast at this time of day," Detective DeLaRosa said.

I assumed she was right; 850 Bryant Street houses not only the Hall of Justice courtrooms but also the San Francisco Jail.

"I'm actually going to call a car service. I know the driver. It may take him a minute if he has another client, but I know he'll come and get me."

DeLeon Davies did not have a client, and he came and got me, and in spite of her glare and knowing grin I managed to say a civil good night and thank you without explaining to Detective DeLaRosa what a life coach does.

As if I knew.

≈🜔≈

DeLeon Davies is, as anyone who knows him will testify, the world's coolest human being. He owns a car service, driving his clients to airports and appointments in order to "stay in touch with my peeps," as he puts it. He also is, as the song says, "a brown-eyed handsome man," with pecan-colored skin and crinkly salt-and-pepper hair pulled back into a short ponytail.

He doesn't need the money that driving nets him; the investments he's made as a result of his conversations with his clients make his home in Piedmont and the Stanford University tuition he pays for his son easily affordable. He just likes the job, likes his clients, and he does the job more capably than anyone else in the world.

"What you doin' at the jail, Miz Xana, you don't mind my askin'?" DeLeon mostly speaks to me in his Oklahoma-rooted accent. With a new client he uses his Yale Graduate School English Professor vocabulary.

I told him the story as he steered the immaculate Escalade across town toward the ocean. I didn't cry very much while I talked. DeLeon contributed an occasional "Well ain't that a muthafucka" along the way, but mostly he just listened, at which he excels, no doubt because of long, dedicated practice.

When I finally fell silent, DeLeon said, "Whatever you need. You understand me? Whatever it is, if there's an earthly way for me to do it, I'm in."

I thought about DeLeon's daughter Netta, who had just graduated from high school. She might have failed to achieve that milestone had not Thorne and I retrieved her, at DeLeon's request and at significant risk, from a violent cult.

By the time I noticed where we were, DeLeon was about to turn left onto 48th Avenue. I had talked the whole thing out, I was both miserable and mad, and I was ready to go to work.

"DeLeon, are you free to help me run a quick errand, and then meet up with Thorne at the café? I need all the brains I can get on this one, and your brain is exceptional."

"All the gray cells are at your service, Miz Xana. I don't have any more clients today, but mostly if you think I can help then that's what I want to do."

"I need to buy a prepaid phone somewhere."

"For the strong, silent himself?"

"Thorne's got one already, I'm betting. I need one for me, so I can talk to Mr. Mum's-The-Word on a phone the police don't know about."

DeLeon thought for a second, and then put the car in gear and aimed us back east on Geary.

Half an hour later I had a no-contract smart phone with 600 minutes of talk time and we were on the way to Daly City, to the East-West Café, the designated meeting place for Thorne and me.

On the way I called Nora and she told me Thorne's new phone number. Saint that she is, she said that she would keep my dogs overnight, that the kids were having a blast with them, and the dogs were chasing various objects all over the house and yard. She told me Hawk with his long stride would get to the toy first, with Kinsey yipping at his heels. Hawk would then trot almost all the way back to whoever threw the toy, and then drop it for Kinsey to bring the rest of the way. Share and share alike, canine-style.

My heart twinged when I hung up; it was getting late in the day and I hadn't told Nora yet that it was Dad in the back yard. The only people who knew the identity of the dead man weren't biological family. Thorne and DeLeon, though, were my "brothers from another mother," and their distance from the biological family would be useful, I was certain. I needed someone who wasn't emotionally hooked into the family, because there were questions I wanted answers to, and I wasn't sure my family members could or would answer them.

Now that it was confirmed that the dead man was my father, was I the only one in the family who believed him to have been dead already? And where on earth had he gone off to during his long absence?

Most important, what had happened to my father that left him in my back yard with a fatal knife wound? Why had someone killed him there and not somewhere else?

Given the circumstances, I didn't think anyone in my biological family was going to want to reply to all these questions, assuming anyone knew the answers.

Their not wanting to answer was just too damn bad.

≂⅂≂

"Can you talk?" I asked Thorne.

"Yes."

"Where are you?"

"The car."

"Where's your client?"

"There isn't one."

"What happened?"

"Stalker's in jail."

"So you can meet me at East-West?"

"In ten."

All in all, a typical exchange with the Prince of Pithiness. If you want to be included in Thorne's small circle of pals you have to accept his taciturnity, and I had lots of other friends who liked to gab if I felt the need for gabbiness.

If Thorne had been a musician like big-band leader Tommy Dorsey, the music would go down and around, whoa-oh-oh, oh-oh-oh, and then it would not come out here.

≈8≈

Rose Sason runs the East-West Café in Daly City, just south of San Francisco. She was born in Manila and moved to the U.S. in her teens, working her way up to owning her own place. Manny, the chef, hails from Guadalajara, and between Rose and Manny the menu fuses lumpia with enchiladas in a generally scrumptious way. The daily menu sports Rose's creative approach to English, and serves as the entertainment portion of the dining experience. The waiting area sign today advertised Swit and Sore Lechon Tacos with Slantro/Corey Andrew.

Thorne, seated with his back to the wall and his glance sweeping across all entrances, raised a hand when I walked in. Not that I would have missed him; it was already late evening, the place had mostly emptied, and at his skyscraper height and about double my weight he was not an entity you fail to notice in any room, crowded or vacant.

To me he looked a little like Howie Long with a Dennis the Menace mop of loose blond hair falling across his forehead.

He stood and came around the table as I walked to him, holding eye contact, and then he had me wrapped up tightly in his arms. I'm not small—at five-foot-nine I'm as tall as many men—but I was dwarfed by this giant who hauled me in to him, and I felt completely safe for the first time all day.

When I sighed and put my hands on his chest, he kissed the top of my head and let me go. He and DeLeon exchanged The Nod, and then engaged in the modern man hug, with handshake and chest-bump-back-slap.

We sat. I put my head in my hands. Without my asking, Roberto the server brought over iced tea, extra lemon, and a glass of ice water for DeLeon, setting them down and walking away after Thorne glanced up at him. Thorne manages to conduct complex conversations without generating any noise.

He lifted his chin at me, the wall sconce lighting up the dark green irises with yellow flecks.

"It's awful," I said.

He waited for me to figure out where to start.

"It's verified that the man who was stabbed in my garden today is my father."

Thorne raised his brown eyebrows until they disappeared under the blond thatch. I had told Thorne a while back that my father was dead years ago, his ashes scattered in the ocean.

"I know. But the ID in the wallet has my father's photo and name on it, and the fingerprints match, and the tattoo is there on his arm. It's him. Thinner and grayer, but him."

"How?"

"I don't see how, but I guess anything's possible," I said.

"Mater?" Thorne was referring to my formidable mother, who is called Mater by everyone in the family, but never to her face.

"I haven't told Mater or any of the siblings yet."

Convening the scattered troops would take some doing, but I realized it was necessary to start the process promptly.

"What's next?" DeLeon said, echoing my thought. "That seems to be the main question."

"I have no idea what to do except tell the family and get them all out here for another funeral. And I don't know what the police will be doing about solving the crime. In spite of my checked-out alibi, I may still be embroiled with them for a while. Oh, and Walt Giapetta told me to tell you to call him as soon as possible," I said to Thorne.

Thorne nodded his head once, and then shook it back and forth in a "No."

"I thought not," I said.

"Maybe. It depends."

"On what?"

"I won't lie. Or get locked up."

Thorne is averse to telling falsehoods the way anaphylactic shock victims are averse to peanuts and shellfish and bee stings. He's equally averse to being locked up.

The detectives would want to speak to Thorne in person, and pin down his whereabouts today, and detain him if they didn't like his answers. They might even find it advantageous to pin a murder on him if no other likely murderer raised a hand and volunteered for the job.

"Can't you hook 'em up with your client and have her alibi you out?" DeLeon asked him.

"Nondisclosure. She doesn't trust anyone to keep her situation confidential, or keep the stalker in prison. I can't tell the cops about her, or refer them to her for my alibi. She'll deny everything and I'll lose her as a referral."

That long speech, atypical of Thorne, meant he was serious. Since Thorne doesn't exactly have a website or TV and bus stop ads touting his services, all his work comes from referrals.

"Oh God I have no idea where to start." I put my hands up over my ears to help hold my brain inside my cranium. "The man in the yard was my Dad. So who was the person who burned up in the car accident all those years ago? Does anybody know what really happened to my father, and where he's been all this time, and why he came back now, and how he wound up stabbed to death in my garden, and why I didn't realize who he was when he called to me last week when I pulled out of the garage and nearly hit him? I thought he was just some homeless guy."

I was shaking, and I felt the heat of tears spilling onto my cheeks. DeLeon reached an arm around my shoulders. He knows Thorne deems shoulder-holding to be a PDA and won't do it. The fact that Thorne had hugged and kissed me when I arrived at the café was an anomaly not to be repeated.

"Shh, shh, baby girl," DeLeon said. "You'll figure it out."

"Bird by bird, Babe."

Thorne, invariably if often unexpectedly literate, was quoting Anne LaMott. Take one step at a time; make slow but steady progress, and you'll get there—wherever "there" is—eventually.

And then the inner voice that calls me "Child" said "Now," and I remembered the cards in my purse. The people who ask me to read their cards are often at wit's end about what to do. The problems they feel stuck about are common enough: family, money, health, job, love.

I was certainly feeling stuck, and this problem certainly fell into the "family" category, and both Thorne and DeLeon were familiar with my reading cards in front of them, so I felt no compunction about pulling out the silk-wrapped bundle until I realized I was in a restaurant.

I got up and walked to the host podium where Rose was marking up the section map for the next morning's servers.

"Rose, with your permission I'd like to use my tarot cards, but not if it's going to disturb you or the other patrons."

I showed her the pack, still inside the scarves. She took a moment to register what I'd said; I doubt she'd heard that same request before. She looked around at the near-empty café, and at where the three of us were seated in the back corner booth. She nodded.

"You go ahead, Xana. If somebody say something I tell them go home if they don't like it."

I thanked her and headed back to the table, pulling up a chair to the open side of the booth's table so my back was facing out to the room and my body was blocking everyone's view. It's ridiculous, in my opinion, but some people are offended by tarot cards, so why offend them if I can avoid it?

I unfolded the scarves and laid them out flat on the table so the cards would sit on top as I dealt. I shuffled the deck until they had physically warmed up. As I was shuffling I took slow, deep breaths in and out and said the prayer I always say when I do a reading: "May the light pass through me undimmed, unrefracted, unaltered."

When I read cards, my training has taught me to allow rather than control the things I say to the Querent—the person I'm reading the cards for. I assert mildly conscious control if I see something alarming or difficult, but I work on staying out of the way of the information my intuition brings forth in response to the colors, numbers, suits, and images. In this case the Querent was me, so anything I intuited was going to surface without my conscious control.

"The Queen of Wands," I heard inside my head.

I sorted through the cards until I found the Queen again, and I set her aside.

When I felt the cards were ready, I cut the deck into three piles.

"The center one," I heard the inner voice direct me. I picked the middle pile up and stacked it on top of the other two.

"I don't remember what I'm reading very well," I said, looking at Thorne and DeLeon. "Since I'm reading for myself, I'm probably going to need your help afterward, to recall what I said and to work through what it might mean."

I've read my own cards with both Thorne and DeLeon, so I was just reminding them to perform the memory-assist. The men exchanged glances, the way men do without saying anything but the glances mean they're ready, and then they looked back at me.

"Seven cards," the inner voice said.

I laid out, from left to right, the Queen of Swords, the Three of Swords, the Eight of Wands, the Emperor reversed, meaning upside-down, the Five of Wands, the Nine of Swords, and the Princess of Swords.

Above them I laid down the Queen of Wands.

She is a blonde, barefoot, crowned and armored woman seated on an orange throne. Her armor is draped in an orange and yellow mantle, and she holds a wooden scepter in one hand and rests her other hand on the head of a leopard lying alongside the throne. Swirling behind her is a pale green windswept sky.

There are seventy-eight cards in the Western-tradition tarot deck, of which fifty-six are suit cards, fourteen cards per suit. The suit cards are the predecessors of the playing cards we use now, but in the tarot deck there are four face cards, two men and two women, instead of the three that show up in the decks people use now to play cribbage or solitaire.

"Sheesh, there's a major message here," I said. "All these Swords and Wands are really screaming at me. Four out of the seven cards are Swords. Swords are about thinking and talking, about ego rather than feeling. Instead of weeping, mourning, expressing love for each other and grieving together, there's going to be a lot of bullshit that may fracture the family, especially the women. Accusations and recriminations and general blaming.

"The Emperor in the middle I'm going to have to come back to, because he's the center card, and the only Major Arcana card. And he's reversed, which is not surprising, but it's also alarming as hell. The Eight of Wands says things are going to move fast—or maybe it means actual movement from one place to another—and it calls for the victory of creativity. It's announcing that creativity is a fulcrum that can shift everything. The Five of Wands is about people figuratively and maybe even literally using their ideas to quarrel with each other, beat each other up. But even creativity and ideas won't stop the distancing and sense of isolation everyone is going to be experiencing. All those swords..."

"What's a Major Arcana?" DeLeon said.

"Besides the suit cards, called the Minor Arcana, there are twenty-two cards that represent the big mysteries of life. Our modern cards are derived from the Minor Arcana. The only Major Arcanum we see in today's playing cards is the first one, the Fool, only now he's called the Joker."

DeLeon nodded that he understood.

I tapped the Queen of Wands. "She's all about inspiration and strength. She loves her life, and she's full of joy and satisfaction because she knows how to harness what others call 'the occult' and master the elements of herself that interfere with warmth and loyalty and fire and vitality. She can frighten some people. Her confidence and independence power her past other people's expectations of what she should be allowed to do. She's never bothered by that, and maybe sometimes she should be, because others can be jealous and even vindictive."

The men exchanged glances. DeLeon lifted his thumb and tilted it toward me. Thorne crossed his eyes, a "Duh" agreement.

I stared at the upside-down Emperor. He sat there in the middle, the linchpin of it all.

"The Emperor card is all about mastery, masculinity, dominance, control, authority, establishing a realm and ruling it. He's also about fathers." I shook my head and picked up the card.

"He's reversed; therefore the control and management and setting of boundaries go out the window. Upside-down like this he's your 'preposterous chaos,'" I said to Thorne, "and he's at the center of everything here."

"Any clues about what you should do?" DeLeon said. "'Cause you the one here, yes?" and he pointed to the Queen of Wands. "All those things you said about her, that sounds like you to me. Where she's sittin', she's able to look at all this from someplace separate, maybe have some perspective."

"I hope so, DeLeon. Yes, she's part of the reading, no matter where I placed the card. She's in the mix, but the reversed Emperor plus all the sword cards can taint everyone's perspective, including mine."

I looked at the Queen and Nine of Swords.

"Those two are about self-imposed widowhood and the guilt that arises from willfully damaging others."

I pointed at the Queen. She holds a bloody sword in one hand, a severed head in the other. The Nine of Swords, in my memory of an earlier tarot deck I had used, showed a robed figure sitting up in bed weeping in the night.

"I have to figure out how intentional widowhood and willful harm are part of this," I said. "Is my mother the cause of it all? Is she the Queen of Swords in this layout? If she is, what happens if I confront her?"

With my elbows on the table I linked my fingers and rested my chin on my intertwined hands.

"I think you have to start with your family, Miz Xana," DeLeon said. "First off, they need to know what's happened, because the answers are likely to start with them. Maybe one of 'em can tell you more about what your Daddy may have been doin', who he used to hang with, somethin' that could aim you in the right direction. Besides, the cops are gonna want to talk to 'em all, see if they can find someplace to get a start on solvin' the murder."

"Whew," I said, gathering the cards and reassembling the deck, squaring the corners and rewrapping them in their silk.

"'Action is eloquence,'" Thorne said. "Bill put that into 'Coriolanus.'"

I shook my head at my man-mountain of a sweetheart who, having quoted some obscure Shakespeare, smiled his barely noticeable smile. If Thorne had ever gone in for a tattoo, "Action is eloquence" would be inked onto him someplace where everyone could see it.

"So I'm going to start acting," I said. "What's first is definitely family phone calls, yes?"

"Or tacos?" Thorne said, the corners of his mouth lifting a tiny bit once more. "Let the rest of the bird-by-bird action wait until you're fed."

I hadn't thought about food, nor had I felt hungry all afternoon and evening. But now, sandwiched between these two most faithful of friends, I realized I was famished.

"Swit and sore tacos sound perfect right now," I said, waving Roberto over.

≍**9**≍

"Get on a plane. Get here first thing tomorrow," I told my oldest brother Brett, who lives in Chicago. I called him while they were making my tacos because he lives where's it's two hours later than the West Coast, and he would be turning in soon, if not already, in order to be up in time to manage his investments in hog futures.

Yes, hog futures. Don't ask me what those are, because Brett is the only one I could ask and he's tried to explain it to me without success. Just buy more bacon so he can stay solvent, is what I took from our Q&A.

"What the hell, Xana," he said in response to the imperative I'd just issued.

"How often have I done this to you?"

There was a pause.

"Well, never."

'And please," I said.

"Okay, if you're going to use the magic word, I'll call you back with my flight information."

My next oldest brother Collin lives in Los Angeles, where he designs things, mostly explosions, for superhero movies. He was between films—which is hard to fathom since cartoon movies appear to have superseded death and taxes as the inevitable constants of modern life—but anyway he agreed to drop the nothing he was currently doing in Santa Monica to hop on a commuter jet in the morning and fly to San Francisco where he would do something, he knew not what, without asking me any preliminary questions.

Nora lives five minutes from my house, and from picking up the dogs she already knew about the murder, so I figured the Bard family jungle drums had been beating nonstop since the afternoon and that was why nobody peppered me with a lot of what's-going-ons.

My baby sister Louisa, aka Lulu, is a fine artist, a landscape painter. She lives in Carmel, where there are a lot of landscapes to paint. Carmel is a two-hour drive from San Francisco unless you drive like I do, in which case it takes ninety minutes. She agreed to pick up my mother from Mater's Pebble Beach house tomorrow morning so they could commute up to the City together.

I didn't trust myself to talk to Mater directly, and Lulu, who is Mater's namesake and gets along with my mother better than any of the rest of us can manage to do, promised to load my mother into a car, via jackhammer if necessary.

Knowing my mother, it might very well be necessary.

≈/O≈

Thorne and I spent the night at the Seal Rock Inn, at the corner of 48th Avenue and Geary, just up the street from my house. I didn't want to risk having the police show up at the house to find Thorne there, so we tolerated a blanket and bedspread made out of unbreathable petroleum products in exchange for an opportunity to work out a more detailed plan, followed by a complimentary full American breakfast in the morning.

The night was clear and warm, with still no sign of coolth or fog. We opened the windows of our corner room and stood with our arms around each other, gazing at the view. We allowed the cypresses and firs of Lands End and the calm black ocean that glittered in the moonlight all the way out past the Farallon Islands to lift the weight of the day from our spirits.

When our breathing had settled, we turned off the lights, stripped, and threw the covers down to the end of the bed. We lay there in the dark, pressed together, face to face, luxuriating in the pleasure of full-length skin on skin. We were quiet, adjusting ourselves, reconnecting hearts and souls if not everything available. Yet.

"Thorne, this one has to be all mine," I said, even though I hated saying it.

"Why?"

"I don't see any way to involve you directly that won't cause you harm."

"Things will change."

"Yes, as I learn more. I'll keep you tuned in, because you'll see everything unemotionally. But the police will be talking to me repeatedly, which means you have to keep your distance."

"Invisibility to the police does not necessarily mean distance from you."

"Sure. But I've been thinking about the cards at the café, especially the Emperor. There's always something for me to learn in any reading, and this one said there's something major that I need to come to terms with, more than just my father's death. Something about establishing my own place in the world, about mastering myself. About conquering fear."

"You're never afraid."

I felt my throat constrict and the sting of tears starting. I took a deep breath and blew it out slowly to release the emotion. I asked myself the question, and heard the answer.

"All those sword cards. People are going to use words as weaponry. They're going to lie to me and to each other. That's going to lead inevitably to loss. To blame and remorse. I think there's a risk of being blackballed by everyone in my family if I pursue this, because the ones who are lying will know they're going to get caught out. Truth always finds a way to be known and acknowledged."

Thorne nodded and his throat rumbled in agreement. Thorne is a big fan of the truth, with its sturdy insistence on becoming known.

"I don't know how to forgive myself for not knowing and welcoming my Dad when he was right in front of me, and this time I've lost him for real. I'm afraid another round of Dad grief won't heal. Or maybe grief doesn't ever heal. It just shifts to stealth mode, looming up like a rogue wave from time to time, flattening you."

I paused and finally spat out my worst fear, in a whisper because this fear was driven by my pitiable and consistent history of watching previous lovers walk out on me.

"And if I let myself be, I'm afraid of losing you, because this whole mess is too much mess, and exposes you to too much risk."

Thorne's arm around my waist pulled me in tighter against him.

"No," he said. "Answers A, B, and C are your call, but not Answer Z. I decide whether Z is a justifiable fear, and it's not and will never be."

He kissed my eyelids, and then my mouth, and there was no more talking about fear and lies and loss.

≈11≈

"Xana, what the hell?"

I was distracted by jumping dogs for a moment as I ignored Brett, commanded Hawk and Kinsey to stay down to no discernible effect, and walked around hugging everyone but Mater, whom I leaned down to air kiss while grabbing the dogs' collars to restrain them. Mater does not like to be "mussed."

I told the bouncing, whimpering canines to sit, and they finally obeyed after I lowered myself into a brown leather club chair. Kinsey settled onto my feet and Hawk leaned heavily against my right leg, his massive jaw resting on my thigh, a reproachful stare directed up at my face. I stroked his mighty noggin in the direction his mother would have licked his puppy head, and he closed his eyes and relaxed.

Brett, as was his custom when in hog futures

mode, had led off the conversation with a peremptory demand and curse when I walked into Nora's living room. He, Collin, Nora, Lulu, and Mater were gathered in the conversation grouping near the hearth, in a room where Ben-Hur's chariot race would be an easy fit. The north wall was floor-to-ceiling glass, but no one was looking at the spectacular view of the Golden Gate.

Nora's international assortment of fifteen biological and adopted kids, ranging in age from three to seventeen, were distributed to day care and schools. The housekeeper was out running errands and buying groceries in bulk, the nanny was in her downstairs chamber, and Hal, Nora's husband, was upstairs in his office. All of which meant the mansion was quiet for the time being.

The living room was reserved for adults, so the plush upholstery and oriental carpets were free of peanut butter smears, Barbies, and X-Wing Fighters.

Nora had put out a platter of turkey and BLT half-sandwiches on what looked like hundred-grain bread, and there was a mound of homemade chocolate chip cookies as well. None of the humans were eating but Kinsey was focused on the broad, glass-topped coffee table in case a sandwich bolted for the freedom of the carpet.

To my mother's consternation, I'm sure, all her children were wearing jeans and sundresses, running shoes and sandals. Mater had opted for what she considered "casual" and was impeccably groomed in a teal St. John knit pantsuit.

After Brett's outburst nobody else charged in with any sort of inquiry, and the room went quiet. I told them the story, and managed to weather the barrage of questions and accusations that interrupted along the way. I watched them all: Brett and Lulu take after our brown-haired, petite mother; Collin and Nora, as am I, are tall and blond like our father.

I'd prepared myself for the onslaught of confusion and doubt when I confirmed that Dad had returned and was the victim in my back yard, but still I felt my stomach clench from the sense of being isolated and attacked.

I focused on breathing, in-out, in-out. I kept my eyes up and alert in spite of the urge to wrap my arms around myself and fold up like a jostled mimosa sprig. This was my family, and I loved them all, but family members can ignore the interpersonal restraint we exert when speaking to non-family, and I had to fight to hold onto my emotional equilibrium.

I was looking and listening for any hint that the news was not news to one of them, especially Mater, who had orchestrated the previous funeral in spite of being divorced from Dad. I was alert for anything besides shock and grief: a knowing glance, a misplaced argument, a comment that demonstrated awareness someone shouldn't have had—anything.

There were dropped jaws and exclamations of

disbelief and horror, incredulous questions, and tears from little Lulu, who leaned into Collin and wept into his embrace, but there was nothing I could identify immediately that raised my suspicions. As far as I could tell, it seemed that my family had been as fooled as I was by my father's previous "death."

"Well then," I said, "if nobody knows where he's been or why we thought he was already dead, we have to decide what to do."

"We have to keep it out of the papers," Mater said, manicured hands clasped in her designer-suited lap, back straight, slender ankles crossed and tucked under the upright chair Hal had brought from the dining room for her. Mater considered bad posture the Antichrist. "Absolutely no scandal," she insisted.

I felt sorry for Mater. This was not the kind of story you dined out on with your Symphony Board cronies. In her society-page crowd, news of this event would be a colossal embarrassment.

"Mother, it's murder," I said.

Collin, kind soul that he is, stepped in to assist in delivering the unwelcome information.

"Mother, I realize that the eleventh commandment in every WASP family is 'Thou Shalt Not Make a Spectacle of Thyself,' but the story was already on the news this morning."

"Plus I acted as next of kin when I identified Dad, so his name has been released," I said. "Some journalist will follow up and discover the previous death. He was a prominent man back then. I don't think there's any way of keeping a lid on this."

"How could you do that? Act as next of kin? I should have been the one called. I'd have delayed the identification until after the initial story died down, so that it was just another murder," Mater said.

I had my mouth open to go after her, but Brett intervened before I could censure Mater about "just another murder."

"Mother, you and Dad are divorced," he said. "You're not next of kin. Xana is the oldest child living here, and the responsibility fell to her, and she fulfilled her responsibility to our father. She did the right thing, and it must have been terrible, for which we all owe her thanks."

Collin and Lulu and Nora nodded their heads, and Lulu, still sheltering in Collin's hug, blew me a kiss.

Mater, as mothers tend to do, loved her first-born son better than her other children, and his rebuke silenced her. Nonetheless, her expression indicated she wasn't happy about it, to the extent that her "youth injections" allowed her forehead to rearrange itself into a micro-frown.

"Are we ready to talk about what to do next?" I said.

"Well," Collin said, "it's not like we have to dig up the unknown father and replace him with the genuine article. Don't we just arrange another cremation and scatter some more ashes?"

Lulu sat up and slapped at Collin's arm.

"Collin, you are forgetting yourself," Mater said.

"On the contrary. I'm remembering that I am my father's son. And I am also remembering that I have a previous supposed father, also deceased. Aren't the police going to want to know more about that at some point? I guess there's not much they can do all these years later, but someone died in that car crash and was cremated, and now nobody knows who it was. And with the ashes at the bottom of the Bay, it's going to be tough to find out."

We were stopped short, and there was silence as we realized there would be not one but two murder investigations embroiling the family.

The chaos had become more preposterous.

"Who were Dad's friends back then?" I asked.

Mater made what for her was a derisive snort. It sounded like a baby chipmunk sniff, and was no doubt intended to convey disgust, but irreproachably.

"What?" I said.

"No one from the firm," she said. "They vanished like vapor when he was let go."

"Why was he let go? They called it a reduction in force, but at the time you said that was just an excuse. Do we know the real reason?"

Mater stared at me, willing me to retract the question. I stared back at her, willing her to answer. She sighed in resignation, perhaps because she never wearied of blaming her ex-husbands for her matrimonial failures.

"He was drunk, of course. He'd been drinking his lunch and was late to an afternoon meeting with an important client. When he fumbled the presentation that was the last straw."

"Who was the client?"

"What earthly difference can that make?"

Something in Mater's tone told me it would in fact make an earthly difference.

"I have no idea what difference it will make. I'm asking questions to see if the answers can be made to pull the pieces into some sort of picture we can understand."

"Alexandra, you are not going to make this another one of your little projects. You poke around where you're not welcome and cause nothing but trouble."

Whence cometh the second source of the long-term therapy bills. The good news is that the therapy did the job, mostly. As Dr. Paul Pelham, "Dr. P.," told me once, "you still have these urges" to cave in when Mater insists that I stop being who I am instead of who she contends I should be in order to satisfy her expectations, "but you no longer act on them."

"Mother, whether or not I am 'welcome,' as you put it, this could not be any more surely my business. I came home yesterday to find my long-lost, presumed-dead father lying murdered and bloody in my garden. *In my garden.* The police confirmed my alibi, but I am betting the detectives still consider me a suspect. I will do everything I can think of to assist the police in learning who killed him. A friend of mine just yesterday told me 'action is eloquence,' and I'm going to act. Now please answer my question. Who was the client?"

It's so seldom that anyone, much less one of her children, challenges her edicts that I believe the shock of it stunned my mother into compliance, even though I'm not her favorite eldest son.

She twisted her mouth into a moue of disgust, postponing her answer, but before she could speak Brett said, "It was Bix Bonebreak."

"That vulgarian," Mater said. Given her mulish dislike of Mr. Bonebreak, I was startled that my father and Bix were even acquainted, much less friends.

"Bix?" I said, looking back and forth between Brett and Mater. She aimed a dagger-infested glare at him and picked up the story.

"Yes. As a favor, because Josiah had asked him to, Bix made an arrangement for your father to represent him in an acquisition. Josiah knew he was on the ropes at the firm, and he thought if he could bring in a new client it would save his job."

Bix Bonebreak owned, among other enterprises, a metal fabrication plant on Folsom Street, south of Market. I'd met him a while back, and he and Thorne had bonded in the way raw-boned he-men sometimes do, in what I'm guessing was an alliance of equal and sovereign powers.

But Mater detested Bix, considering him uncouth, a word rarely used anymore but a favorite slur of Mrs. Louisa Duncan Livingston Monaghan Bard, the often-married-but-never-happily former debutante belle of Darien, Connecticut.

"How were Dad and Bix friends?"

"I don't believe they were, really." Mater made the barely distinguishable chipmunk noise.

"Sure they were friends. They played squash at the club," Brett said. When Mater glared at him, he shrugged. "I saw Bix with Dad a couple of times when I was there taking tennis lessons. I could hear them talking and laughing in the locker room when I was changing into my whites."

"Were there any other friends or confidants?"

I looked around at everyone. They looked at each other and then back at me, and shook their heads no.

"Mother?"

"No one of whom I'm aware." She looked down at her carefully tended fingers, stretching them out to examine her expensively twinkling rings.

We were all silent. I think we were just stumped about what to do about everything. I looked around at my siblings in an unspoken question, and Brett took charge.

"Let's give it a rest for now. It's been a shock for everybody and we need some time. We can

think about next steps and reconvene at dinnertime to decide."

Everyone agreed, in my case with relief that
the conflict the tarot had predicted was over for
the time being. The rest of the family meeting was
devoted to arranging housing for three siblings,
whom I could accommodate, and Mater, whom
Nora would put up, until we could hold another
funeral.

Before we split up to get people moved into
their rooms, I told everyone that I would let Walt
Giapetta know where folks were so he could in-
terview them, and Mater made the sniffing chipmunk noise again.

I drove home with Collin and Lulu seated in
the back of my beloved Chrysler 300C. Hawk was
hogging the middle of the back seat and en-
croaching on some of my siblings' window seat
space. Kinsey was curled up in front by Brett's
feet.

It occurred to me that Brett had known about
Bix's final favor to Dad. Had Mater told him
about that? Had Dad? I thought about Bix and
wondered how close he and my Dad had been
back then. Those two questions weren't much to
work with, but it was someplace to start.

Two blocks from my house the car began to
shimmy even though I was cruising at an almost
legal thirty miles per hour. I slowed, thinking
maybe a wheel had come loose, and then I saw
the suspended traffic signal at 48th and Geary

swinging wildly in the breezeless afternoon of the second hot, humid day in a row. I pulled over and stopped at the curb. Even stopped, the big sedan continued to tremble.

And then my two-ton vehicle containing six hundred pounds of occupants hopped into the air and bounced back down to the left of where it had sat idling. Hawk's head hit the roof liner and he yelped, as did the rest of us. Collin put his arms around the massive dog and held him.

Because in this "fucking earthquake weather" we had just experienced a major earthquake. One of the San Andreas fault's tectonic plates had subducted, causing the earth above it to swell and fall like an ocean wave does, lifting and dropping everything in its path. The 1989 Loma Prieta quake had ended with a mighty whip crack of the ground itself. That epicenter was 80 miles away from the Bay Area, and yet that long shaking and final swell-and-drop caused the Marina District's landfill to liquefy, and the Bay Bridge and Nimitz Freeway to collapse, killing dozens and injuring hundreds.

My house rests on a cliff a few hundred yards away from the San Andreas Fault. I looked around at my brothers and sister and asked in a shuddering voice if everyone was all right.

"Shit, Xana," Collin said. "That one wasn't kidding."

They were born in the Bay Area, and two of them still live in California, so the occasional earthquake doesn't shock them; even so, this was not a typical shaker. Lulu and Collin were holding hands across Hawk's chest, their knuckles tight and white. I was glad the airbag hadn't deployed when the car dropped back onto terra not-so-firma. But Collin and Lulu were all right, Brett was all right, the dogs were all right, and I was all right.

What I couldn't be certain about was whether my house was all right. I needed to get home to see if there was anything still standing.

⇌12⇌

Yes, the house was still standing, although as soon as the Genie lowered the garage door behind the car all the lights went out. I groped my way to the side door and opened it so sunlight could show everyone the way to the stairs up into the house proper.

The power grid for the entire City had been shut off, as it always is in a natural disaster of the magnitude we'd just experienced. Sirens wailed intermittently throughout the ensuing evening as emergency personnel tackled the damage to structures and humans.

As all responsible San Franciscans are, I was prepared with candles, flashlights, bottled water, and battery-powered radio (actually my cell phone, tuned to the Internet channel for the emergency station). The quake had caused some car accidents and structural damage to older masonry and stucco buildings, but no freeways or bridges had collapsed and there were no fatalities. Our task was to wait it out until power was restored and the rubble was cleared.

Brett used the landline to call Nora (he sat for more than a minute until a dial tone finally beeped), to be sure she and her family were unhurt and to reschedule our meeting for tomorrow. I did a walkthrough of the house, opening all the windows as I went to let out the heat and using a flashlight in rooms where the sun couldn't reach.

I found nothing alarming except for a plus-sign fracture across the dining room ceiling; the fissures ran from the four perimeters to the chandelier in the center. Apparently the earthquake's final P-wave had cracked the whip strongly enough that the violent jerk nearly yanked the chandelier out of the ceiling and down onto the table.

Downstairs in the dark garage there was mail, a padded envelope and some direct mail flyers, in the metal basket suspended from the slot in the garage door. I picked the items up and, after checking Thorne's apartment for damage, carried the mail back upstairs to the kitchen island to look through later. I kept walking through the house, finishing up on the third floor. Except for plaster cracks in a couple of rooms, everything seemed to have survived.

The back yard and dog run were still festooned with yellow police tape, so the dogs couldn't go out there and neither could I, but in any case I sorely wanted some time with the other Dr. P., my nickname for the Pacific Ocean.

I find my hours spent by the ocean to be as, if not more, effective (and certainly less expensive) than time spent with the human Dr. P. Given the stresses of the previous two days, I wanted to unload everything on the maritime Dr. P. as soon as I could.

I leashed the dogs and we headed out for a long amble—no striding heartily in this heat— down the hill to Ocean Beach. Brett, Collin, and Lulu tagged along, the four of us pairing up and then walking solo, enjoying the rare shirtsleeve evening in San Francisco and catching up with each other.

The dogs wanted to be let go so they could romp, but I kept them leashed. Ocean Beach is a national park and it isn't legal to let the dogs run loose there. I didn't want to ignore the rules and devote my attention to monitoring them in case a park ranger showed up; this was family time and I wanted to devote my attention to my brothers and sister.

"What's up with you?" I asked Brett, handing him Hawk's leash.

"You're the one with the news," he said. "Same-old same-old for me."

"Everything going well with the porcine side of things?"

"As long as forty-thousand-pound contracts of frozen pork bellies get traded every day, day-in-day-out, my world is a good world," he said.

"Are you seeing anyone?"

I asked because Brett remains single, in spite of his dedication to all things pig. I'm sure you're as stunned by that news as we all are.

"I was dating a very nice Korean woman, but after a few weeks I made the mistake of letting her cook me dinner at my place. It was like she set off a culinary weapon of mass destruction."

"I see. How was the food?"

"The beef with hot sauce and tomatoes was delicious, but I'm serious. Every pan, every bowl, every utensil, every cooking surface, the oven, the sink, the walls, the floor—for fuck's sake, even the cabinet handles. I'd say the ceiling too, but I was afraid to look up. Xana, you know me. It's not like I require a sterile environment, but I gave up and called a cleaning service. They added a surcharge to the original estimate because of 'unanticipated out-of-norm labor charges related to kitchen.'"

"So eat at her place. Or order in. Or go to restaurants. I mean, did you like her?"

"Of course I liked her, but that dinner turned out to be a showstopper. I had to keep fending her off about repeating the dinner experience. She thought I didn't like her cooking, which I didn't. I mean, I liked the taste of the food well enough, but the process was a killer. The kitchen would always look like a ten-person food fight had been happening in there since Reagan was Governor."

Brett was making chopping motions with his

hands, like he was calling the runner safe at third on a close play, or crying "No mas," like Roberto Duran.

"Okay then."

We walked for a little in silence.

"What else do you know about Dad after the divorce?" I said.

My big brother looked sideways at me. He sighed and shrugged his shoulders.

"We talked now and then. He gave me investing advice, and recommended me to some of his contacts in Chicago. That's how I wound up there, doing what I'm doing. Dad was moving increasingly toward commodities rather than pure financials. He said it was safer when you dealt with actual, physical stuff rather than just money. Physical stuff can have inherent value. He thought money was becoming 'a construct rather than a reality,' were his words, and he didn't trust it. 'Too many crooks spoil the math,' he said."

"When was the last time you talked to him?"

He looked away from me toward the ocean, thinking for a moment.

"Maybe two years before the accident? He called, and he was kind of on a rant about gold, of all things. I think he was probably drunk, because he wasn't making a lot of sense. Gold and gold mining and gold investments are a pretty uninteresting area, if you ask me."

This, from the pig products devoté.

"Anyway, I kind of cut him off and that's the

last time I spoke to him. I never got a chance to..."

Brett's face bloomed red, and he rubbed his nose and sniffed. No matter how old you are, your parents are your parents.

I took his arm and pulled him next to me. We adjusted our strides to match each other and walked companionably for a few yards.

"I'm going to check in with Collin," he said, avoiding eye contact and shoving Hawk's leash into my hand.

Lulu joined me, taking Kinsey's leash. Hawk is almost as big as Lulu is, so I could hardly fault her choice of dogs.

"Are we going to meet Goliath?" she said.

Mater and Nora have met Thorne, and have apparently been communicating with the rest of the family about his exterior dimensions.

"I don't know. Thorne won't be any place where there are going to be police, so until Dad's murder is solved he's not likely to be at the house. Certainly not until after the crime scene tape comes down."

Lulu asked a series of questions about him: Who were his parents, where did he grow up, what schools did he go to, how did he earn his living, etc. Of the five of us, she's the closest to my mother, living near her, bearing her name, and mimicking some of her affectations, one of which is asking "qualifying questions" about people.

The intent is to classify and assort folks into "us" and "them," and I find it obnoxious, so I gave the vaguest possible answers: he's not close to his parents; Back East; an assortment of Preps and Ivies; personal security, and then I changed the subject.

"How are the art sales going?"

Lulu looked at me and smiled, indicating that she was perfectly capable of spotting a change of subject when she encountered one.

"The economy is up, and real estate is hot again, so the galleries are able to move their merchandise. You've seen what I paint. It's commercial, with trees and flowers and deer, and that's what people want to put up over the sofa in their second home on the eighth fairway at Spanish Bay. Anyway, my stuff sells pretty steadily."

"Lulu, your paintings are wonderful. There's more than just lovely scenery. There's emotion in there. The feeling you capture is why people buy them."

"You sweetheart. And the ankle is all better?"

She hooked her arm through mine and squeezed us closer together.

"It is. No pain, no arthritis, no problem with movement. Just a miracle."

I had broken my ankle into little bitty bits not long ago, and after the orthopedic surgeons were done making it bionic I'd done a lot to regain as close to full functionality as humanly possible. I was grateful every day that I could stand up and walk.

"That's great to hear. I know you threw the

book at it, with surgery and physical therapy and Reiki and massage and acupuncture. Good job, Sis."

We were quiet until we were almost to the Beach Chalet, when Lulu spoke again.

"Dad called me just before he died," she said. "The first time, I mean."

I kept walking, even though I wanted to stop and stare at her. Lulu was close to Mater, not Dad, and I had never imagined he would reach out to her; I was supposed to be Dad's favorite. I felt a pang of what I was afraid might be jealousy.

"What did he say?" I was careful to keep accusation out of my tone.

"He was ranting about crazy stuff. I really couldn't follow him. Something about going to the Sierras, and to Nevada. I remember he said 'Winnemucca,' because seriously, how could you forget a name like that?"

"Why did he want to go there, of all places?"

"Did Brett tell you about the gold?"

Now I stopped and turned, looking Lulu in the face.

"Dad told both of you about that?"

She looked up at me, he head tilted to the side.

"Why wouldn't he?"

Brett and Collin caught up to us. I turned to Collin.

"Did you talk to Dad before the car accident?"

"Yes...?" He dragged the word out so that it

became a question.

"What about?"

"Oh Jeez, it was a long time ago."

"Please, Collin. Anything."

He thought for a moment, turning to stare at the calm ocean that stretched away westward all the way to Asia.

"Hmmm. The most I can come up with is something about going away for a while. I think he said he'd figured something out that was going to change everything, something about gold of all things, and that if I had to find him I should call Bix. I wrote it off as more of the same stuff he pulled when he was under the influence. You remember how he was."

I think my chin might have been trembling. Collin put his hand on my shoulder.

"I wonder if Nora heard from him, too," I said.

"She did," Brett said.

"So I am officially the cheese standing alone, here? Because I never got a call."

Collin and Brett and Lulu exchanged looks. Collin got elected, maybe because he already had his hand on my shoulder and physical intervention was anticipated.

"Xana honey, we assumed he talked to you. We didn't mention anything to you because, well, you were kind of touchy about him. We thought if he'd talked to us, he had to have talked to you. You and he were always so tight."

"Except I stopped speaking to him. I got an unlisted number. He was always drunk and I couldn't handle it." I shook my head. "Wouldn't."

Another wave of grief broke over me and I felt my face crumple into the ugly cry. Collin put his arm around my shoulder, Brett stepped to the other side of me and put his arm around the other shoulder, and Lulu stepped in front to reach around my waist and hug me. Hawk barked, and Kinsey whiffled and yipped.

The image of the Emperor card flashed into my mind, with his link to all things paternal, and to the reversed Emperor in my reading the previous night at the café. In my mind's eye I saw the heavy bright gold crown he wore. Finally I pulled myself together.

"God," I said, pulling a tissue out of my pocket and cleaning up my face. "How did we all turn out to be such decent human beings? Sorry. What I really mean is I love you all."

"Sure you do. As long as I don't violate the WASP commandment forbidding me to confuse my fish fork with my salad fork," Collin said.

We laughed, the rueful laugh that appreciates the person who defuses an overload of emotion, and turned around to walk back up the hill to the house. We didn't talk much as the sun grew oranger and settled down in the unblemished sky toward the Prussian blue water.

The air was cooler down at sea level where we'd strolled the esplanade a few steps from the frigid Pacific, but still there was no discernable breeze. The endless horizon meant no fog would be rolling in to chill the evening air and bring relief from the day's sultriness.

There was almost no traffic along the Great Highway parallel to the beach. People were staying home tonight, no doubt sobered by the quake and glad to be with their families. I was glad to be with mine.

Back at the house I got the sibs settled in: Lulu with me in the master bedroom; Brett and Collin split up into the guest room and bedroom/office. Collin was on an inflated double mattress. Stymied momentarily when we realized the boxed bed would require manual inflation during the power outage, I remembered the car-cigarette-lighter-powered tire inflator I kept on a garage shelf but had never used, and we managed to get the bed blown up to full size that way. I let the men wrestle the thing up two flights of stairs to the third floor.

"Of course they should carry it. They have the upper body strength," Mater would have said.

So Collin was set up in the office, surrounded by plywood plank tabletops holding computer equipment. All the keyboards and monitors made him feel right at home, although the technology might as well have been rocks until the power was restored.

Towels were laid out and everyone had gone through Kitchen Orientation. They could make their own breakfast as long as breakfast didn't require electricity.

The gas stove worked (if we lit the electronic ignition burners with matches), which meant coffee could be managed for those who like that sort of thing.

I'm a tea drinker, and boiling water is pretty much the extent of my cooking expertise, hence the Kitchen Orientation. Thorne keeps the fridge stocked, so food was no problem except for spoilage. Everyone was encouraged to keep the refrigerator door closed unless necessary.

At sundown Collin foraged briefly, pulling a couple of boxed pizzas out of the freezer and putting them in the oven. It took us a minute with the butane pistol lighter to get the oven burner lit, but the Y-chromosome crew seemed to enjoy that sort of problem-solving, what with crawling around the cork floor armed with mitts and screwdrivers to lever the metal oven surfaces around and get the lighter to the gas element.

"We make fire," Collin said upon arising from the floor, his lower jaw jutting out, waving his oven-mitted and betooled hands. Brett opened his mouth wide and roared like Simba.

Lulu tossed a salad. I dialed the iPod to Craig Monticone for what DeLeon called "bookstore music" and set the table using the good china and stemware because pizza with sibs warrants an upscale ambience.

We ate by candlelight under the useless chandelier, nobody talking much. It had been a difficult day all around, and there would be more tough days ahead. I've learned that grief is weird and unpredictable in its manifestations and duration. The cards I'd read at the café said weird unpredictable grief-driven happenings were likely.

I think we all wanted to avoid saying or doing anything that would fracture the family any further in the wake of this second round of paternal death.

After dinner Collin called Santa Monica to talk with his partner, Shane, and assure him everyone was safe. The two men have been together for four or five years now, and Collin appears to have figured out how to keep the relationship solid. As bullied as he was in high school, it's a joy to see him so comfortable with himself—so happy—as an adult.

There were only candles, no Wi-Fi or TV or sufficient light to play cards or a game by, and none of us wanted to talk about Dad. After hugging each other good night, off we marched to bed.

I awoke somewhere around two a.m. to the hum of the refrigerator kicking on; my bedroom is above the kitchen. Light from the street lamps at 48th and Anza glinted around the hems of the curtains. Lulu, undisturbed, slept on, curled away from me on the far side of the king-size bed, her breathing steady and quiet.

I checked my temporary cell phone where it

lay plugged in on the nightstand. The charging symbol was lit. There was a text from Thorne: *Here*.

I smiled and went back to sleep. The morning would be busy, and maybe difficult, and maybe I would need Thorne to be actually here instead of *Here*.

I hoped so.

⪜*13*⪜

"I'm afraid there's bad news, Xana," Brett said. He was standing at the kitchen island, his sturdy compact body dressed in Dockers, loafers without socks, and a short-sleeved knit shirt. His brown hair was combed smooth, and he held a mug of coffee in his left hand.

"Oh yummy, bad news is just what I was hoping for first thing in the morning," I said, plugging in the electric kettle to heat tea water. I stood there in my cotton caftan and slippers staring at the kettle, willing it to boil.

"I was up early so I took the dogs out," he said. Given that Brett gets up at 5 a.m. Central Time in order to monitor and manage his hog futures realm, he was more than likely going to be awake pre-dawn Pacific Time.

"Thank you," I said, meaning the dog walk.

"Of course. Anyway, I walked into the park with the pooches, and on the way back I saw that there was a crack in your foundation."

"What?"

"Yeah. Actually there are two cracks. Kind of big ones. One's on the side facing the park, and a sort of matching one is on the other side facing your neighbor. I'm not tall enough to see over your garden fence to check if there are any cracks on the ocean side of the house. Maybe you could ask the police for access to your yard so you can take a look."

"Oh man, what else?"

I lifted my hands up and dropped them in frustration. That Emperor card again, with his meanings of established boundaries and solid fundaments on which a life could reside securely. Reversed, he apparently means a cracked foundation.

"Didn't you have the house earthquake-proofed? And don't you have earthquake insurance?"

I imagine Brett has insurance on his insurance.

"Earthquake insurance is a scam," Collin said, strolling languidly into the kitchen wearing black leather slippers and a teal and magenta silk robe sashed at the waist. He was carrying Katana, one of my two black cats. Katana hides from everyone, but I guess today was a new day, feline-wise. My shy kitty was flopped along Collin's forearm, his legs dangling down on either side, and his head rested on Collin's fist while Collin sat himself down at the island and stroked the length of the cat's back. The cat was purring so loudly it sounded like an apnea-sufferer's snoring.

"Well aren't you all Bindi Irwin this morning," Brett said. "Where did you capture the wildlife?"

"The cats found me," Collin said. "They slept with me last night. They undoubtedly sensed how fond I am of pussies."

There would have been universal spit takes if any of us had had liquid in our mouths, or maybe we would have kept ourselves in check. Collin maintained a straight face and without comment Brett opened a cupboard to pull out a coffee mug for his younger brother. I spooned loose Earl Grey tea leaves into a little yellow ceramic pot and poured boiling water in. Brett put another mug on the island for me. I sat down at the island and stared at the pot while the tea steeped.

"Why is earthquake insurance a scam?" I asked Collin.

"Because in a really big one the insurance company will just go bankrupt and you'll never see a dime. That's what happens after a disaster. After Mississippi floods, after Andrew or Katrina or Sandy or Matthew, after tornadoes, after the sky rains pianos or there's a zombie apocalypse, any of that shit, the insurance companies claim 'Act of God' and walk away. You might as well plunk your earthquake insurance premium into a savings account and earn some miniscule interest while you wait for Armageddon."

"How are you coming up with this theory?" Brett said.

"It's not a theory. I saw it on the Internet, so it must be true."

"Oh," I said. "Of course."

We all nodded.

"Meanwhile," I said, "Brett tells me the house's foundation is cracked. A while back I got the framing bolted to the foundation, so the house shouldn't slide off the cliff in a quake."

Collin made a "you wish" gesture with his free hand.

"Or at least it shouldn't slide off easily. But I don't even know where to start to get the foundation repaired. I think I'll have to call my handyman, Marvin, and see if he knows what to do. Maybe you just mix up some special foundation goop and shove it into the cracks with a spatula and voilà! Everything is tickety-boo."

Both of my brothers live in condos, so home repair is not their forte. As if it were mine.

"There's probably a special kind of foundation spatula," Collin said. "Some hybrid metal-rubber thingy, like Wolverine would have. I could call Hugh Jackman up and ask. Please say I should call Hugh Jackman and discuss latex-coated Adamantium spatulas."

"I bet Amazon would have one if Mr. Jackman declines to take your call," Brett said.

Lulu walked in wearing a pink fluffy terry-cloth robe and Dearfoam slippers upholstered in leopard-pattern fake fur.

"Amazon has everything," she said. "But do they have breakfast?"

"Coming up," Brett said. "I found bacon in the freezer."

"Of course you did, dear," Collin said, opening the cupboard for a coffee mug. "I think you just have to say 'Abra-ca-Porkra' and bacon materializes in front of you."

As we were putting together the food, Lulu asked about a neighbor across the street, a woman who was arrested recently for a double murder.

"Didn't you turn her in?" she said.

"Well, sort of. I called 9-1-1 when her dog dropped a human foot in front of me. Apparently Agatha came home one morning and found her husband in bed with his secretary, so she shot them both, cut them up, and buried the pieces in her back yard."

"Oh, haven't we all," Collin said.

ה ה ה

Between the four of us—well, more like the three of us plus trusty setter-of-table me—we had vegetable frittata, home fries with onions and peppers, biscuits slathered with butter and honey, stewed tomatoes, fresh orange juice and a platter of bacon. I thought about bolting the doors to the outside world and never allowing my brothers and sister to leave me.

But I was gracious; I did not prevent them from getting showered and dressed while I rinsed and stacked the dishes in the dishwasher. Since schools were canceled for the day while engineers checked the buildings for damage, and therefore the proliferation of children would be everywhere at the mansion in Sea Cliff, Brett had arranged for Nora and Mater to come over to my house at nine-thirty for our follow-up family meeting.

In the meantime I needed to tour the foundation damage and call Marvin the handyman. I wanted to talk to Bix Bonebreak about his friendship with Dad, but I was leery of calling him, thinking maybe it would be better to just show up at the Folsom Street plant and brazen my way into Bix's office, as I'd done once or twice before. I think Bix appreciates brazenness in lieu of the courtesy of a phone call for an appointment. I'd have to check with Thorne to get a he-man's perspective on the brazen v. courteous approach.

I went upstairs to dress in something Mater would find inappropriate for a woman of my background and breeding.

≈14≈

The family meeting took much less time than I'd imagined it would. The news had settled in overnight, it seemed, and everyone was ready to reach accord and move ahead without contention. Even Mater, in her Ferragamos and de la Renta silk Mikado frock, was compliant.

She told Brett what had been arranged the first time, and Brett got on the phone and scheduled a duplicate cremation and ash-scattering, to be conducted as soon as the medical examiner released the body.

I called Walt Giapetta to ask about that, and when I told him my family was with me he instructed me to keep them there until he and Detective DeLaRosa could arrive.

Within twenty minutes the detectives rang the doorbell. They separated us and asked the others individually for their whereabouts at the estimated time of the murder, and Detective DeLaRosa wrote everything down, including the names and numbers of corroborating witnesses.

That was that, except that Walt wanted to know if I'd heard from Thorne. I told him I had, that I'd asked Mr. Ardall to call Walt right away, that I'd given Mr. Ardall the detective's number, and so the ball was in Mr. Ardall's court. Walt gave me a look, but he let the matter go.

Just as well.

≶15≶

"Thanks for agreeing to see me. I'm here because I want to ask what you know about what happened with my father."

I knew from experience there was no point to small talk with Bix Bonebreak, so I skipped over asking about his family or his opinion of the pennant race.

Six-four, granite-solid, hatchet-faced, rough-skinned, with a face the color of your breath on a cold morning, Bix tilted his head to stare at me out of eyes the black-brown color of mushroom spores. He didn't glower, but I felt the physicality of his gaze assessing me.

"I agreed to see you because I like you," he said, "in spite of your unfortunate choice in mothers."

I felt my face redden. I stared back at him, refusing to look away from his dominating gaze. Years ago my mother had managed to foil the youthful romance between her friend DeDe Iron-house and a younger, poorer Bix, on the basis that Bix was too crude to tolerate or be trainable. DeDe and Bix had each married others, and thereafter carried dampered torches. DeDe was now widowed, but Bix wasn't; the sting of the lost love remained sharp and the torch burned steadily, but Bix was a man who took a vow and honored it.

Faint sounds of screeching metal being cut and machined came through the wall of his vast office where we sat above the production line of the steel fabrication plant on Folsom Street. The aircraft-carrier deck of a desk hulked between us in the center of the room. A four-cushion gray chenille sofa, polished steel coffee table and arm-chairs that would be a comfortable fit for a silver-back gorilla sat against one wall. On the opposite wall was a conference table for ten with padded leather executive chairs. Thin, gunmetal-gray carpet squares covered the floor.

"Unlike your mother, you shoot straight," Bix said, "and like your Dad, you keep going even when somebody's squaring off against you."

"Somebody like you, for instance?"

He laughed, if the short harsh bark that broke out of him could be classified as a laugh.

"Like me, yeah. You do take after Josh." Bix paused. "I saw the news."

"Did you know he was still alive all this time?"

He waited, deciding. But Bix always opted for straight-shooting.

"I did."

I shook my head and blew out a puff of air in frustration.

"Xana, we were friends since we were kids, and he had good reason for what he did."

"You may think so. I can't imagine any reason good enough to mislead his family for all these years."

"You'd written him off, remember? All of you gave him the boot."

"You have no right to reproach us. He was a drunk. He was impossible. He was unsafe to be around. He refused to get help. You have no idea what my family went through before we each, individually, made the decision to cut him off. He blacked out while smoking in bed and set my guest room on fire."

I heard myself getting louder as I spoke.

Bix put his palms up, holding me off from adding more to the litany of paternal misdeeds. He stood up from the chair that allowed him to sit up higher than the person across from him and came around his gigantic desk to sit next to me in the other molded metal visitor chair. He leaned forward and rested his elbows on his knees, clasping his hands in front of him. He was making himself nearer and smaller, the way big men do when they want to disarm a lesser, perhaps wounded, adversary.

"I'm sorry. You're right. He was a mess. But he was a friend to me when I started out, and back then I really needed one. So when he needed me to be his friend, I stood by him."

I took a deep breath and calmed down.

"How is it you two became friends? I mean, you seem so dissimilar."

"On the surface, maybe."

He grinned at me and shook his head at a memory.

"How were you similar under the surface, then?"

I couldn't help myself. I wanted to hear a contemporary's perspective on my Dad.

"Well, think about it. He was the go-to investment banker for the metallurgical industry, back and forth to Pittsburgh and East Chicago and Ontario before it all mostly moved offshore. He lived here because of your mother, but he spent all his time in Mexico and Suriname and Angola and anyplace else in the world where there were new smelters to be built. He was the guy negotiating with post-colonial governments about sharing infrastructure development costs like roads and dams and bridges in exchange for the mining and plant and foundry and mill jobs that would result. Hell, they sent him to Russia to talk to those clowns about building a smelter somewhere in Siberia. They were doing preliminary research into using kaolin clay, which they have a lot of apparently, to produce aluminum instead of bauxite, which is the ore everybody's used for aluminum so far. Between his hollow leg for vodka and his loathing for criminals, Josh was the only guy who could not only keep up with those assholes but beat them at their own game."

I took that information in.

"I remember that. He said the people he was dealing with were all crooks."

"Yep. He turned down that Russian deal because as soon as you built the smelter and perfected the technology the Russians would kick you out and steal everything, so why bother?"

"That sounds exactly like him."

"That was him. No matter what happened to your father later, you should keep in mind what a smart, determined, honest guy he was to begin with."

Bix patted the chair arm with the palm of his hand as he spelled out each of my Dad's characteristics.

I nodded and said, "Thanks."

We sat for a minute, remembering that man, the guy before the incurable drunk who faked his own death.

"What do you know about what happened to him? Where did he go for all these years?"

"I only know some of it. There came a point when he wouldn't tell me any more about what he was up to."

"I'll take anything I can get here. I need to know why someone would kill him, and not just kill him but do it at my house. I'm going to stay in the police crosshairs until the murderer is found."

"Do you know about what happened at the bank?"

"I know you were involved in a meeting that went south."

"He had an acquisition he wanted me to take a look at. If it hadn't been a solid idea I wouldn't have gone along with it, but he'd identified a little foundry that was going through a rough period, and I was interested in expanding from straight fabrication to castings. So I agreed to a meeting down at the bank, purely for show since I was already planning to move ahead. Josh wanted the partners to see him as a rainmaker, so we were going to go through the motions in front of them."

"But he blew it."

"He did. I couldn't help him after that."

"Did you go ahead with the deal?"

"I did, but with a different partner, a guy named Jeremy McDunnigan."

I winced. After Dad was fired I had heard of Jeremy McDunnigan from my mother. She didn't flatter him in her description, but then Mater's flattery is mostly reserved for friends' designer clothing, holes-in-one at the Monterey Peninsula Country Club, and the champagne brunch at the Clift Hotel.

"Xana," Bix explained in response to my wince, "I'd already signed an agreement with

Josh, and therefore the bank. The agreement was binding, even if your Dad wasn't the partner who actually proceeded to manage the acquisition."

"Meanwhile, what happened to my father?"

"When the meeting became impossible, I walked out. I didn't make a big deal out of it. I just got up and left. I knew Josh was screwed, and that there was nothing I could do in that moment or afterward to help him."

"You couldn't have spoken up?"

"Xana, he fell down, dead drunk, walking into the conference room. If I'd stayed the other partners would have known we were working something together. I called Josh the next morning to see what, if anything, I could do to pull things back together for him. He told me he'd blacked out and couldn't even remember what had happened; he just knew he was fired. So I'm sorry, but there was nothing I could do. I know you know how that goes, because you've been fired. There comes a point where you realize there's nothing you can do."

I sat, accepting the truth of what Bix was saying. Yes, the truth still hurt, in spite of my winning a lawsuit and a lot of compensatory cash.

"What caused him to disappear, though, and fake his own death? Why would he do that?"

"I only saw him once after he was fired. He went dark on everybody, me included. I tried calling him multiple times, but it always went to voice mail and he never called back. When I finally did get a call from him it was a huge relief. I was afraid the booze had taken him."

I nodded to encourage Bix to keep talking.

"We arranged to meet down at the Marina Green after dark. We sat there facing the water, and he told me about how the firm had ripped him off, stiffing him on the bonus he was due for as a partner, and that this guy McDunnigan had stepped into his shoes at the bank and was stealing his clients and his investment strategies."

"Was Dad sober?"

"He said he was. I couldn't smell alcohol, so I decided to believe him, at least for that one night. But he definitely looked down on his luck. It was cold there, the way it gets by the Bay at night, and he didn't have a jacket on. I wound up giving him mine."

"What investment strategies did he say McDunnigan stole?"

"Oh Jeez, I don't know if I remember. What does it matter now?"

"I don't know that it does. But Brett told me something about Dad getting all fired up about gold. I'm just poking around until I can figure out how to put the pieces together in a way that makes sense." I looked up at Bix. "If they ever will."

I shrugged. Bix looked down and thought for a moment.

"Josh did say something about gold to me, now that you mention it. And he said he was going to have to play dead."

"Did he explain?"

"Just that he had to disappear so that no one would come looking for him."

"Why would anyone want to look for him?"

"Xana, your guess is as good as mine. I will say that, at the time anyway, I thought your Dad was more than a little paranoid, and after his troubles with booze and then getting fired and divorced and estranged from you kids, I was taking what he told me with a pretty sizeable grain of salt."

"Why didn't you tell any of us about this?"

"Because I gave Josh my word that I wouldn't. Now that he's gone—killed—well, I think under the circumstances I'm released from the promise."

Bix held his gaze steady on me, knowing I would understand, and I did. In the world my Dad and Bix operated in, your word was everything. I remembered Dad's admonition about dealing with crooks: A crook was anybody who couldn't be trusted to keep his word.

"Since that one last deal, have you had any further dealings with the bank, or with Jeremy McDunnigan?" I asked.

"No. I didn't like the guy. I especially didn't like him after what Josh told me about him."

"Do you know anything else about what my Dad intended to do, or where he was planning to go? Or anything about what he meant to do with gold?"

"No. Well, maybe. I have this vague idea that he said something about Nevada. Some guy in Winnemucca he needed to meet."

Bix paused and then sighed heavily.

"I gave him five thousand dollars," he said.

"Just like that?"

"Just like that."

"Because?"

"Because he asked for it, and I had it to give, and I knew he wouldn't have asked unless he needed it and had nowhere else to go for it."

I sat back in my chair, chastened by the realization that Dad couldn't come to his family for help. Bix must have thought I was annoyed at him for giving my father the money.

"Xana, Josh gave me my start. Without him I would not be here today. I didn't come from old money like your family did. I was a sports scholarship kid at school with your Dad, and we became friends in spite of the sniping he took from the snooty shit-nosed classmates about his hanging out with me, the slum-dweller jock. You know, I'd have given him ten times five thousand dollars if he'd asked for it. We drove here and I pulled the money out of the safe. He handed me back my jacket, shook my hand, and walked out."

"Did you ever find out what happened to him after that? Did you ever get your money back?"

"I never heard from Josh again. I never expected to see the money returned. I never knew what happened to him until I saw the news of the car crash. I figured that was the fake death he'd been planning. And now you've got his real death to deal with. You have my condolences, Xana."

He reached across the space between us, put his big meaty hand on my shoulder and squeezed. I put my hand on top of his, feeling the sandpapery skin, and then stood up to go.

"Will you let me know what you find?" he asked, standing up and walking to the office door to let me out. "Because you're like him, and that makes me believe you're going to stick with this until you find out what happened."

I told him I would and thanked him for seeing me. He wished me luck.

From the car I called Thorne on the burner phone.

"Road trip tomorrow," I said. "I'll call with a schedule, after I take care of some local chores. We're about to embark on some 'action is eloquence' stuff."

"Headed to?"

"Winnemucca. In Nevada. Although I doubt there's another Winnemucca anywhere."

"A lifelong dream," Thorne said.

≈*16*≈

There was too much to do all of a sudden, but I was determined to wrestle some of the preposterous chaos into a manageable array of tasks that actual humans could accomplish via eloquent action.

On the ride across town toward home I thought through the items on the list: I needed to meet with Jeremy McDunnigan about the bank's dealings with my Dad, assuming Mr. McDunnigan would agree to meet, and assuming he would agree to tell me anything.

I had to check in with Walt Giapetta about the case and whether the crime scene tape could come down, but avoid admitting that I planned to leave California to go poking around in Nevada. Walt would tell me I was certainly not welcome to go poking around anywhere near the murder investigation, and even more certainly not in some-place out of state.

I needed to talk to my family about what eve-ryone wanted to do until the coroner released my father's body. Did they want to stay and wait, or go home and return for the funeral, the date for which was TBD?

I had to arrange for pet-sitting while I was away in Nevada, unless my siblings were plan-ning on staying with me until the repeat burial service. If so, I had to find out if they were willing to tend to the abundance of zoology sharing the house with them.

I had to do research on whatever went on in Winnemucca that would have drawn my Dad there almost ten years ago. And even though Winnemucca was a straight shot eastward across Interstate 80, it was a sizable town, as towns in Nevada go that aren't Reno or Vegas. I was hop-ing I could identify likely places for elderly peo-ple to gather and reminisce.

I imagined seedy bars with cactus motifs and a row of aging nickel slots squatting along the back wall, with an equally seedy row of seniors on barstools who would be happy to have me buy them all a round, after which they would remem-ber, with startling clarity and in immense detail, my father and what he'd been up to a decade ago.

Hey—it could happen.

I had to talk to Marvin the handyman to see if he could tackle the foundation repair.

I wanted to check out what, if anything, had been noted all those years ago about the car crash my father was supposed to have died in. Were there any clues about who the actual deceased person might have been?

When I got back to the house I realized there was one more task I'd forgotten: yesterday's mail was sitting on the kitchen island. I heard Lulu and Collin talking upstairs in the office, and the leashes and dogs were gone so I guessed Brett had volunteered for dog-walking duty again, like the good soldier that he is.

I pulled the scissors out of the kitchen drawer to slit open the padded envelope and, multitasking, reached for the house phone to call Walt. I had the handset scrunched between my shoulder and my ear as I slid the contents of the envelope out onto the countertop.

I dropped the phone. The battery cover flew off when the handset bounced against the edge of the counter and hit the floor. I listened to the far-away dial tone, and then the voice announcing that I should hang the phone up, and then the penetrating off-hook screech you could still hear if you were fifteen miles across the Bay in Oakland.

"Xana?" Lulu called downstairs.

"I've got it," I shouted, returning to planet Earth. I picked up the phone to silence it. "Sorry."

"Xana—Your Eyes Only," was on the cover letter, the words in my father's handwriting.

Behind the cover letter there was a scrawled note on its own piece of paper. Behind the note was a will, its pages stapled together multiple times across the top of the document with a sheet of blue paper attached at the back.

I flipped through the few pages; there weren't many. The will was a fill-in-the-blanks form like you could download and print from online or buy at an office supply store. The last page was dated and signed and witnessed. I didn't recognize the witnesses' names. I flipped back to the second piece of paper and read the handwritten note.

Xana, give this to your attorney. If you don't have one, ask Bix Bonebreak to refer you to someone you can trust.

My previous will went through probate, and what little estate remained at that time was settled, and that's the right way to have handled everything after the car crash. But now the situation is different, and so here is a new will.

I want you and your brothers and sisters to know that I always loved you very much, and I ask your forgiveness for not being a better father to you.

You'll see that I did my best to make amends to you all for my many faults. You will think I haven't done enough, and you'll be right.

I don't know where everyone is anymore, but last week I found you. So I'm relying on you to do the right thing by your brothers and sisters.

I always remembered your birthday, Alexandra. I hope you have remembered mine.

Love, Dad.

I scanned the will and read that my Dad had left everything to me. I found the box of tissues and yanked a few out of the box to hold up to my eyes. Losing my father once had been hard enough; losing him twice was a bastard; reading that he loved me and had given me all that he had left took me straight back to the day a week or so ago when I had seen him and failed to know him.

I sat and let the tears fall for some minutes. When they stopped I wiped my eyes and nose and tossed the damp tissues into the garbage.

I looked over the note and the will more carefully, and it occurred to me that there was just one snag in Dad's estate planning: I had no idea what "everything" consisted of, or where on earth I was supposed to find it.

≈17≈

I ruled out telling my siblings about Dad's will just yet. I wanted to wait until I found out what was being willed. I folded the pages up and put them in my purse. I threw the padded envelope into the trash.

People, no matter how sane and centered they are, can act very differently from their sane and centered selves when they're grieving. Throw in the possibility of cash in any quantity, and behaviors can torque into such awfulness that there's no working your way back to normalcy.

I recalled all the Sword and Wand cards in the reading at the café, with their message of dispute and lost tempers and figurative if not literal decapitation, so I kept my mouth shut. I would tell my family once I knew what the actual outcome was of the will, and not before. If they were going to lose their minds, let them go berserk once and for all about actual facts, rather than dragging out and chewing over conjectures endlessly while we tried to determine what was really at stake. If I couldn't find out what Dad meant us to inherit, I would never mention the will at all. What would be the point?

Brett came upstairs with the dogs and I asked him about Dad's former employer, and whether the investment bank had gone under during the 2008 crash. He told me the bank had been bought and was now renamed and operating as a boutique firm catering to the high-tech industry. From the time Microsoft first ruled the tech universe, the pattern of growth for such companies has been slanted toward acquiring their competitors rather than developing the new killer app themselves.

I found the new name—Franciscan Frères— and called, wondering why they would decide that the new company name should make them sound like their employees were walking around in robes and cowls instead of pinstripes—but then money is a religion to most of the folks who work in investment banks.

After navigating the phone tree and employee directory, I finally reached Jeremy McDunnigan's voice mail and left a message asking for an appointment. I said it was in regard to the estate of Josiah Wayfield Bard, because I thought Jeremy would need a compelling reason to agree to talk to me, and in my experience the only thing that compels bankers is the prospect of more wealth, preferably someone else's that they might potentially grab a slice of.

Walt Giapetta, when I spoke to him next, expressed his sympathy in response to the cracked foundation news, and told me the crime scene tape would probably come down within another day or two. He agreed to see about sending an officer over to escort me into the garden so I could see if there was any additional earthquake damage to my house.

Walt estimated that Dad's body wouldn't be released to us for another couple of days at a minimum; the medical examiner was backed up. When I asked if there was any news about the case, he told me he couldn't discuss it.

I thought about mentioning the envelope and the will to Walt but decided against it. I was already a person of interest in the murder; if Walt learned that I was my father's sole heir, despite my not having the faintest idea what I was the sole heir of, the rule of "who benefits?" that all detectives have drilled into them from their first moment on the job would no doubt cause him to haul me off to jail charged with some version of homicide.

Marvin the handyman agreed to come by in the early afternoon, and he assured me he could handle the foundation repair. He said repairing a foundation crack was probably no big deal unless the house had slipped off the foundation entirely, in which case he was not the guy for the job. He'd need a hammer and chisel, some mortar mixed with an acrylic bonding agent, a trowel, a bucket, and a big sponge. That's all the repair would require, he told me, and he could complete the work in a few hours. He'd take care of patching and painting the indoor plaster cracks, too.

I love Marvin.

My brothers and sister, upon learning that it would be another few days at least before we could conduct a funeral, elected to stay in San Francisco until then.

"It's a family confab," Brett said. "We need to bond with Nora's new kids anyway. And as long as I have a phone and my laptop I can work anywhere, really."

"You have awesome machinery upstairs," Collin said. "Just fucking awesome. Lulu and I are designing together and we want to keep going with it. Meanwhile, where did you get all that equipment? I didn't know you were all that tech-savvy. You have literally got a state-of-the-art setup in your guest room."

"I think His Hugeness may have played a design and development role," Lulu answered him, looking up at me and nodding.

I nodded back. "Yes, Thorne bought all of the computers and peripherals. But I am a dab hand at FreeCell on my iPad. I go out nearly every time."

≈*18*≈

The phone rang. It was Jeremy McDunnigan, returning my call, or rather his assistant was returning it for him, and I was put on hold after confirming who I was. I didn't know anyone did that anymore, have an assistant place calls to ensure that Mr. Honcho didn't have to waste time pressing buttons or sitting on hold until the desired party was on the line. Apparently some ancient traditions are still honored in the world of high finance.

"Miss Bard?" Jeremy said, once we were connected. I was tempted to ask him to hold for me, but my siblings were all eavesdropping shamelessly so I kept myself in check.

"Mr. McDunnigan," I answered, not answering him.

"You're Josiah's daughter?"

"I am."

"I was sorry to see the news about him. My condolences."

I heard reticence and perhaps curiosity in his tone.

"Thank you. Yes. It was shocking."

We were silent. Now that I had him on the phone and my brothers and sister were listening, I wasn't sure what I wanted to do with him.

"May I ask what led you to call me?" he said at last.

I pulled myself together and started talking.

"As I mentioned, I'd like to make an appointment to discuss a number of matters with you. There are issues regarding my father's estate that require resolution, and the issues date back to his time with the previous incarnation of your bank. When you and he were both partners."

I was bluffing. Brett and Collin and Lulu were looking at me funny. I turned, averting my eyes, and held up a "Wait-a-sec-and-I'll-tell-you-when-I'm-off-the-phone" finger.

"When would you like to meet?" Jeremy said. "I can clear my calendar if necessary."

Well, that was a surprise. Why would this mighty *macher* clear his calendar for the non-client daughter of a long-gone former partner? I pushed to see what it would get me.

"Are you free for lunch today?" I said, looking at the clock, with its hands closing in on noon. I listened to Jeremy McDunnigan breathing.

"I think it would be best to have this conversation away from the bank," I added, when the silence dragged on.

I don't know why I added that. I think maybe I was afraid that once we started talking he would tell me something that would make me start crying again. If I was in a public place I thought I could manage to keep my emotions in check. "Thou Shalt Not Make a Spectacle of Thyself" would rein me in.

"Let's say one o'clock at Tadich," he said.

"I'll see you there."

I ended the call and put down the phone.

"Well, that was weird," Brett said.

"More than I can tell you," I agreed.

"Who was that, and why are you going to lunch with him?" Collin said.

I told them about my meeting with Bix, and Bix's mention of Jeremy McDunnigan's usurpation of Dad's clients.

"But that was so long ago," Lulu said. "What does all that matter now?"

"I don't know that it does. But why did he call me back so quickly? And why, as soon as I mentioned 'issues with the estate,' did he agree to clear his calendar and have lunch with me right now? Something isn't right."

"Meanwhile, what estate?" Brett said.

"Exactly. Does he know something we don't?" I said.

"So what are you going to do?" Collin said.

"I am going to drive downtown to the Tadich Grill where I will have a nice shrimp Louis salad and see what I can get Jeremy McDunnigan to tell me. I have no idea what that might be. I'm just going to ask a lot of questions and see what he says."

"Wear the magic jacket," Collin said.

He was referring to my red leather jacket. Strangers walk up to me and blab their deepest secrets when I wear that jacket. I have zero idea why that is. Maybe some truth-telling pheromone that's released by the red leather dye wafts over people's psyches and runs the "blurt-all" launch codes.

"Good idea," I said. I realized it was still hot outside, so the jacket would just be there for the pheromone power.

"We're coming along," Brett said.

"No."

"Not to sit with you. Just to be there in the restaurant. To keep an eye on things and make sure you're safe."

"Why wouldn't I be safe?"

"Also to have lunch," Collin said. "I haven't been to Tadich in ages. I need cursory but excellent service from a highly competent but slightly disdainful waiter who brings me a plateful of perfectly sautéed rainbow trout."

"Scallops," said Lulu.

"Sourdough and butter," Brett said. "Chicago is a sourdough wasteland."

I went upstairs and, conscious of the stubbornly equatorial weather, changed into a pale pink linen boat-necked shift and red linen ballet slippers. I pulled the red leather jacket out of the hall closet, slung it over my arm, and headed toward the steps down to the garage.

"One second," I said, and ran back upstairs to my room.

"You're not," Lulu said, looking at the high-heeled taupe leather strappy sandals I was carrying when I came back down.

"I am. I'm going to put them on right when we get to the restaurant. I want to be as tall as possible with this guy."

"But you're going to be sitting the whole time," Brett said.

"Not when I get there, and not when we leave. These guys are all about power, and height is power. I'm going to use any advantage I can get in this meeting. The dress is to look like a woman of leisure, the jacket is to get him to tell Mama all, and the shoes are for intimidation."

"To what end, though?" Brett said.

"I haven't the faintest."

"Well, at least you aren't going into battle unarmed," Collin said. "Those shoes are fabulous. Much higher heels than he'll be wearing. Well, maybe not—this is San Francisco, after all."

"What about your ankle?" Lulu said.

"I am going to trust in bionicity," I said, "and I'm only going to walk about twenty feet in these things, because any more would be suicidal."

We loaded ourselves into my vastly cherished Chrysler 300C and drove down to the financial district to see what Jeremy McDunnigan knew that I didn't. Which was likely to be a lot, I thought, if I could manage to pry it loose from him using the combined powers of red-leather pheromones and shoe-generated altitude.

≈14≈

The perennially crowded Tadich Grill, on California Street in the heart of the Financial District, has been a local dining establishment since Gold Rush days. The great food and the unique atmosphere combine to make it popular every day, all day, from the time it opens at 11:30 a.m. until well after the downtown area clears its commuters out at the end of office hours.

I waited while the line of people in front of me gave their names to the host before they stepped aside to wait to be called. The long, tall, narrow room, with its half-paneled walls, had small curtained rooms holding tables for six along the left side and a very long counter with individual seating along the right. In the remaining floor space there were linen-draped tables for two and four. The kitchen stretched across the back wall.

At the podium I said I was meeting Jeremy McDunnigan and the host, pulling out two menus, gestured to a man leaning against the wall who pulled himself upright and held out his hand for me to shake. I took it, matched the pressure of his grip, and was pleased to see that I was looking down at him thanks to my footwear. With the high-heeled sandals on I stood over six feet, and Jeremy McDunnigan didn't. A momentary frown creased his forehead.

"I'd have recognized you," he said, forcing a smile. "You look like Josh."

He held his hand out, palm up, gesturing for me to follow the host. We threaded our way along the narrow aisle to a table along the left side of the restaurant. I sat down facing the street, and saw my siblings queued up waiting to give their names to the host upon his return to the podium. Both Jeremy and I put our jackets across the backs of our chairs. He was wearing a white-on-white striped dress shirt with a tie in shades of cornflower and daffodil.

"Thank you for agreeing to meet with me," I said.

"My pleasure."

A prompt waiter in a starched white jacket appeared and took our drink orders: iced tea for me, tonic water on ice for Jeremy. I wondered if Jeremy had held back on adding gin or vodka to the tonic. His pale skin was clear, but there was what looked like a permanent flush across his nose and cheeks. I had seen that flush on my Dad's face when he was drinking. Maybe Jeremy had already helped himself to a dram of Stoly or Sapphire before he left his office for our lunch. If so, all the better. A lot of drinkers talk more than they should. I hoped Jeremy was that sort of drinker.

We sat, smiling politely at each other. He looked to be fifty-ish, with a receding hairline of graying mouse-brown strands combed carefully across as many bald spots as they could manage to cover. His thin lips cut across his lower face in a wide gash, under a long, high-bridged nose flanked by deep frown lines. His forehead was lined with permanent horizontal creases, and his wide-set eyes the color of dull pennies looked out at me from under eyebrows that were starting to caterpillar away from him into Sam Waterston/ Eugene Levy territory.

"Shall we order before we discuss what led to your call?" he said.

"That sounds good."

We studied our menus, printed anew each day, even though I knew what I wanted and I suspect Jeremy knew what he would order as well.

When the waiter returned with our drinks we ordered, as he expected us to do. If we hadn't been ready, the waiter would have disappeared for longer than we'd have liked, having dismissed us as tourists unfamiliar with the correct drill—or, much worse, lovers who would linger over the table making goo-goo eyes and playing footsie, eventually leaving a tip that didn't account for the lost turnover revenue.

Tadich's white-jacketed waiters are admirably competent; they materialize and dematerialize exactly when they should during the course of your meal. They do not endorse or decry your food choice, they are never chatty, and they don't announce their names because you won't need to know a name. If you need your waiter, he—and they are all male— materializes without having to be summoned via arm-wave or name-calling.

Our drinks in hand, our menus swept up and gone, I looked at Jeremy and he looked at me. From tarot readings I've learned to wait, to let the other person fill in the uncomfortable silence.

"Again, I'm so sorry to hear the news about your father," he said.

"Thank you."

"Do you mind telling me what happened?"

"I'm sure the news covered the basics. He was found, stabbed to death, out by Sutro Park."

I left out the part about it being at my house, in my garden. I wanted to find out how much homework Jeremy had done. Another long pause elapsed.

"I must say, it was quite a surprise," he said.

"Yes. A shock for all of us."

"Had he been in touch?"

There was a momentary flicker in Jeremy's

eyes as he asked. Without looking down he turned his fork over, resting it on the tines, and then over again onto its curved bowl. I realized Jeremy was driving the conversation, imagining he was in control of it, happy to be in control of it.

"No. Not since the car accident."

I didn't mention Dad's contact with Bix.

Our food arrived quickly, as it usually does at Tadich, and we stopped talking while the waiter set it down and asked if there was anything else we needed. We declined, and he dematerialized.

"Do the police have any suspects?" Jeremy said, squeezing lemon onto his petrale sole.

"Well, none except for me, I think."

He stopped mid-squeeze and looked at me. The caterpillar eyebrows lifted.

"Dad was found in my yard."

Jeremy set the squashed lemon wedge onto the rim of his plate and rested his palms on the cloth on either side of it—an observant WASP, honoring another commandment: "Thou Shalt Not Place Thine Elbows Upon the Table."

"In your yard? How did that happen?" He'd taken a moment to phrase his question.

"I haven't the slightest idea."

We were silent. Jeremy picked up his fork again and took a bite of fish. I took a bite of shrimp and Louis dressing and lettuce. I'm sure it was delicious, the lettuce chilled, the tiny shrimp plump and fresh and tender, but I have no recollection of tasting it. We chewed.

"What have the police done so far?" he said, after swallowing.

"Nothing they're telling me anything about."

We poked our forks at our food. I looked up and saw Brett, Lulu, and Collin being seated two tables away. Collin flexed his arms into a body-builder pose, encouraging me to be strong. I looked down at my salad, hoping I'd kept my face unchanged and that Jeremy hadn't seen me register anything.

But he had. He turned to look, but Brett and Lulu were the ones facing him with their eyes averted and they look like my mother, not my father. Plus there was a couple at the next table blocking Jeremy's full view, so he turned back around.

"Someone you know?" Jeremy asked.

"From when I worked downtown a few years ago," I said. "It's a small city."

"Yes."

He looked thoughtful, his fork resting upside-down along the edge of his plate, his fish and steamed broccoli ignored.

"Miss Bard, why are we having lunch?"

The tarnished-copper eyes focused on mine, and I thought that any alcohol he might have imbibed had worn off. Here was the shark, sniffing for blood in the water, tiers of pointy serrated teeth lined up and sharpened.

"It's Xana, please."

I smiled. I was going for naïveté. I have found

that a woman in a summer frock pretending to be clueless is often taken to be actually clueless, and cluelessness is often dismissed as harmlessness.

"Xana, you called me for a reason."

"Well, as you know, I'm sure, when my Dad died before? He left almost no estate. I mean, there was really nothing."

Jeremy nodded. I was looking down and up, away from and then into his focused stare. I was mimicking someone thinking about what she was saying, not hiding anything, just a scatterbrain trying her darnedest to be methodical, orderly.

"But at the time, because Dad was estranged from the family, we didn't really investigate the situation. Because of all that had happened, we assumed there was nothing. I mean, there was a will and everything, and it was put through probate by Dad's attorney, but there were no assets that we could find, so we basically let the matter rest."

I looked up. Jeremy nodded.

"Well, now it's been almost ten years, and he shows up again, and someone has murdered him. My father was a very astute man financially. Well, of course, if anyone would know that, you would know that. Anyway, what if in these last few years he was able to assemble a few assets? I thought since you were once his partner, you might have been in contact with him. You could have some information for the family about Dad's current situation. Or perhaps you helped him. Just because he was an old friend."

"Ah." Jeremy looked down at his cooling fish.

"Because why would anyone murder my Dad?" I said, and Jeremy looked up at me again, a level, assessing stare.

"What reason could anyone have?" I went on. "And, I don't know, I thought perhaps it might have been about money? I knew from my mother that you had been the one to assume management responsibility for my father's accounts, and I thought that if anyone at the bank could be helpful with information about Dad or his financials, it would be you. I mean, how could he just disappear for so long without anyone knowing? And because if there turned out to be an estate of any kind this time, even if Dad didn't write a new will, the remaining assets would be awarded to his children. My sister could use any inheritance that came her way, even a small one."

Lulu was doing perfectly fine without an unanticipated inheritance, but I shrugged and shook my head—the clueless, harmless daughter, wasting this important banker's time wondering about something too silly for smart people to wonder about.

The waiter materialized and asked if we were finished. Jeremy, without asking me, told him we were. The waiter looked at the amount of food left on our plates and asked if we wanted boxes to take anything home. We declined and he picked up the plates and silverware, stacked them with the butter and lemon dishes on his left arm, and disappeared.

Jeremy smiled. He leaned back and put one palm on the cleared tablecloth. His face shifted to a bland smile of confidence, maybe even smugness.

"Miss Bard—Xana—I'm afraid I can't help you. I haven't seen or heard from your father since the day he left the bank."

He turned his palm over in a show of innocence. I didn't believe him, but I nodded and sat back, the picture of resignation.

"Well then, I guess that's all I can do. I'll have to let the police figure this out. It's just so frustrating not to know where Dad's been all this time, or what he's been doing."

"You don't know?" The shark was circling again.

"Not the faintest."

The waiter materialized, asking if we wanted coffee or dessert as he placed dessert menus on the tablecloth in front of us. When we said no he dropped the check and picked up the menus.

I reached for the bill, but Jeremy pulled it away.

"Please. As a courtesy, because of your Dad."

I agreed, smiling as dim-wittedly as possible. Jeremy opened his wallet and put down actual cash instead of a card. This lunch was not going on an expense account, and there would be no record of it.

"Thank you for agreeing to see me on such short notice, and thank you so much for the delicious lunch," I said.

"Again, it has been my privilege. Josh was my mentor, and I owe him a great deal. I only wish the circumstances today were less difficult. Please let me know when your father's service will be. I know many of his former colleagues will want to be there."

I didn't believe that would be true at all, any more than I believed anything else Jeremy had said. We stood and picked up our jackets, and I was glad to see Jeremy frownno when he had to look up at me. He put his arm out to guide me to the front, but I excused myself and pointed to the stairway behind me that led up to the restrooms.

"It's a long drive across town," I said. "Thanks again."

I turned and tottered gingerly to the stairs, watching as Jeremy went out the front door and turned right. He crossed the wide window facing California Street on his way back to Montgomery Street and his office.

≈20≈

I'd have picked up my abandoned but full iced tea glass except the busser had already cleared the table and reset it for the next patrons. I moved two tables closer to the front window and sat next to Collin, pulling off the perilous sandals as soon as my rear end was safely on the seat.

"And?" Brett said.

"Did the magic jacket work?" Collin said.

"Not especially. Although something's there. I couldn't tell you what, exactly, but something."

"Did you eat anything? It looked like you didn't eat," Lulu said.

"I couldn't eat. I focused on being an idiot, and it turns out I can't be an idiot and chew salad at the same time."

A waiter materialized, the same one who had served Jeremy and me two tables over. I ordered iced tea and a shrimp Louis salad. The waiter made no comment. This is San Francisco, where the weird and their weird requests are ubiquitous, and he was noncommittally excellent at his job. In moments he rematerialized with iced tea.

"So why do you think something is there with this guy?" Brett said. Broken sourdough bread crusts sat next to his lunch of Sterling pork chops.

"Because he asked all the questions," I said.

"Why wouldn't he? Some voice from the distant past calls from out of nowhere and wants to meet right away. Wouldn't you want to find out why?"

"It was more than that. He was trying to figure out how much I knew."

"Which is exactly zip," said Collin.

"Exactly."

"So what did you talk about?" Lulu said. She was cutting her scallops into tiny bites, making them last.

"I wondered out loud if Dad might have, in the intervening years since his first death, figured out a way to acquire an estate. And I wondered whether Jeremy, as a former partner, might have helped Dad do that."

Cutlery was dropped. Sibling stares were aimed at me. Food was ignored. I was grateful the restaurant had emptied out a little and there was no one at the table immediately to our left.

"Xana, where the fuck did that idea come from?" Brett said.

"Why not?" I said. "It's been a long time. Dad could have done anything. He could have sobered up. He could have rebuilt his investments. Jeremy could have helped him without realizing the family didn't know what was going on."

"Why would he help Dad? I thought he was this young Turk who jumped right in and stole all of Dad's accounts," Lulu said.

"He's not young anymore, and I'm sure he has made it his business to guard his accumulated turf like a wolverine. Meanwhile, I don't know."

I took a chance on changing the subject.

"Please, guys, I just want to eat, okay? I was sitting with a shark just a minute ago and I didn't dare eat while he was sharpening his teeth at me. Or he's a wolverine. Or whatever. Some crafty, predatory animal ready to pounce and bite down hard enough to sever something essential. So please. We can talk about this more on the ride home."

The waiter materialized with my salad and asked if there was anything else I needed. I shook my head no. The lettuce was chilled and the tiny shrimp were plump and fresh and tender. We talked about what Collin and Lulu were designing in the upstairs office and how many frozen pork bellies Brett had managed to trade that morning, and intended to trade after we got home.

I picked up the check.

"Please," I said. "As a courtesy. Because we're all here for Dad."

≈21≈

When we got back to the house Marvin was there, standing at the Sutro Park side of the house next to a widened foundation crack. His chisel and hammer lay on the ground next to a sponge and a pail of water. Marvin was using a power drill and a long drill bit attachment to mix up some thick goop in a five-gallon bucket.

After introducing Marvin to my brothers and sister, who all shook his gnarled, callused hand, I told him an officer might be by to let him into the back yard. Marvin winked at me from under his white straw cowboy hat brim.

"I'll look when he gets here, Miss Bard, but not because I'll need to."

Marvin is old-school. Police officers are all men, and women are all "Miss."

"You rascal. You ducked under the tape."

Marvin winked again. "Not so's you'd notice. And there's nothing back there to mend, so I'm all set. This'll take me an hour or two, and the cracks in the house'll be another couple 'a hours. Cissy'll send you the ticket at the end of the month."

Cissy was Marvin's wife, and she lived up in Clearlake. His paying customers were in San Francisco, so he spent weekdays in the City and drove home on weekends.

I thanked him, and asked him to let me know when he was done so I could call off the law if an officer hadn't yet showed up. Marvin said he would and turned back to his repair work.

In the house, I explained my travel plans to Brett and Collin and Lulu.

"Why do you have to go all the way to the middle of Nevada?" Brett said.

"Because it's the only clue I've got about where Dad might have gone after the accident."

"How can you expect anyone to remember him from so long ago?" Lulu said.

"I don't. I'm following the only clue I've got, even if it's probably not going to get me any-where."

"We can go with you," Collin said, "and share the driving."

"No need, thanks."

"Ah," he said. "Out on the highway with the Colossus of Roads."

"I think I get that, and it's so awful I think I want an apology," I said. "But I'm going to ask you guys to take care of the dogs and cats, so I think I'm the one who has to apologize."

"We'll take care of everything here. Don't you worry," Lulu said. Brett nodded.

"I'm guessing there's a WASP commandment here somewhere," Collin said. "'Thou Shalt Have No Kibble Before Thy Kitties Have Kibble.' Or maybe that's only a commandment on Facebook."

I hugged them and pulled out my burner phone to invoke the Colossus.

≈22≈

"See if DeLeon will drive," Thorne said.

We were at the East-West Café, having an early dinner, planning our probable boondoggle. The foundation and plaster cracks were mended, the indoor paint touched up over the dried spackle, and my brothers and sister were going to have dinner with Nora and family. I thought of the Emperor card's solid foundation, and was glad that mine was literally if not figuratively restored.

"Why?" I said. "I can drive. You can drive, even if you have no license."

"DeLeon knows about gold," Thorne said.

"You know about gold. You have the money bin full of it."

"Bought and sold in small amounts. Not as a financial instrument."

"I feel like it's going to be an imposition on

him. Yes, he's a better driver than both of us put together, and he knows about gold. But still."

"Call him."

So I called DeLeon, explained what had been going on so far and where Thorne and I were headed. I didn't ask him to go along; I left the information out there to see what DeLeon would do. Being DeLeon, he figured out the unspoken request instantly.

"I'm in, like I told you I would be. It sounds like this is what that card was talking about."

"Which card?"

"The one with all the sticks flyin'."

"Eight of Wands. Sudden, unforeseen movement. DeLeon, you have to tell me if this is going to be any kind of too much to ask."

"I'm lookin' forward to the change," he said, "even if I'll still be drivin'. If it helps you find out what happened to your Daddy, I want to be one of the ones doin' the helpin', you feel me? Terrell can handle the clients. School hasn't started up yet."

Terrell was DeLeon's son, who filled in with the car service when he wasn't engineering something very intelligent at Stanford.

We agreed it would have to be an overnight trip, since the travel time was going to take between six and seven hours just for driving, plus stops for meals and fuel. So it was early the next morning that Thorne and I drove across the Bay Bridge to Piedmont, a wealthy suburb nestled in the Oakland hills, to pick up DeLeon and head out from there.

It took a little over three hours to drive from Piedmont to Reno, where we stopped to fuel up and find an early lunch. I'd brought a bunch of CDs to shuffle through the multi-disc changer: Bonnie Raitt, Beverley Knight, Kenny Rankin, Chris Stapleton, Gretchen Wilson, Adele, Benny Goodman, Steve Postell, Ella Fitzgerald, Amos Lee. The music playing over the car's exceptional sound system kept conversation to a minimum.

The good news is that the speed limit once you hit Nevada is mostly seventy-five, which is just as well when you get past Reno and Sparks, because the desert landscape is pretty uniformly desolate and gray-beige as Interstate 80 tracks alongside the Truckee River. You want to get through it as quickly as possible, so we were doing eighty-five. Well, more like ninety. In the Chrysler with its mighty engine it felt like forty.

Every so often there were little blurts of habitation alongside to the highway; many of them—Patrick, Derby Dam—too small to warrant an exit ramp of their own. Past Fernley the road takes a sharp turn from eastward to northeastward, curving toward Utah.

There was a mostly unpopulated rest area at Gilpin and we stopped to stretch our legs and use the bathrooms. When we got back to the car my cell phone sang Mater's assigned ringtone: "She Drives Me Crazy." Thorne and DeLeon, who both know my mother and her ringtone, stepped back out of the car and put what they imagined was a safe distance between themselves and the imminent cataclysm.

I knew I had to answer the phone; there's no use putting off the inevitability of Mater. As soon as I answered the call some more preposterous chaos devolved.

"Xana, where are you? Brett says you're somewhere with that Goliath of yours." Mater's tone was even more brittle than usual.

"Hello, Mother. What's going on?"

"You have to come home this instant, do you hear me? It's an emergency."

I've learned from experience that Mater's definition of an emergency does not always gibe with regular humans' definition. But with my father having been murdered just three days previous to this conversation, I thought Mater's word choice might actually be accurate, so I clarified.

"What's happened? Is everyone all right?"

"It's DeDe."

"Oh, no. Has there been an accident? Is she hurt?"

"Oh good heavens, nothing like that. It's worse. She's been in touch with that vile man."

"What vile man?"

I was slow on the uptake, given that I'd met with the vile man the day before.

"You know exactly who I mean. That awful Bix Bonebreak."

I took a deep breath. It had been more than thirty years since Mater broke up the romance between Bix and DeDe, so I was having trouble aligning the word "emergency" with "DeDe has been in touch with Bix."

"Mother, seriously, you have got to be kidding. How is this an emergency in any way, shape or form?"

"Because she kept it from me. I had to hear about it from Ann. I wouldn't have known if Ann hadn't let it slip. She thought I knew. DeDe's been keeping it a *secret* from me."

"Given your attitude, that's hardly a surprise. Again, Mother, I'm not seeing the emergency here."

"His wife has cancer. Pancreatic cancer. *Incurable cancer.*"

To the extent that she ever raised her voice, Mater was doing her version of a banshee shriek. I held the phone away from my ear and pointed to it, looking over at Thorne and DeLeon and shaking my head. They shrugged the "like-we-can-do-anything-about-it" shrug.

I put the phone back to my ear.

"Well, I'm very sorry to hear that Mrs. Bonebreak is so ill. That's dreadful news. No wonder Bix's friends are calling to offer support."

"Alexandra, you are purposely being obtuse. DeDe is a widow. He will be a widower. He has money now, but that has not made him any less of a boor."

"Okay, Mother. Reading between the lines here, you are concerned that DeDe and Bix will rekindle their romance and you don't like the idea. I get that. I'm alarmed at your lack of compassion for Mrs. Bonebreak, and for Bix and his family for that matter. But I certainly don't see this as an emergency that requires my immediate attention."

"But it is. You know him. You've spoken to him. You're friends with DeDe. You're out on some fruitless quest, poking your nose into matters that are none of your affair, keeping company with those unsuitable friends of yours. You should come home where you belong and discuss this with DeDe and that awful man. You can make them understand how ridiculous it will be for them to resurrect any sort of relationship after all this time."

A flash of insight flew through my roadnumbed brain: Mater was worried about her socialite quartet, consisting of DeDe, plus Charlotte Swansdon and Ann Donner. She hobnobbed—and made large donations with—this wealthy clique in order to get priority seating at the symphony and opera openings each September. She abhorred the thought that they would end up forced to incorporate Bix the Barbarian into the couples-only events. Mater, currently divorced, went to such soirées accompanied by a meticulously well-mannered, well-dressed man known in her circle as a "walker."

"Mother, we'll talk about this when I get home, probably tomorrow or the day after. In the meantime I'll think about what to do."

I was stalling, hoping she would calm down in the intervening day. There was no point explaining right then that my thinking about what to do would result in my resolving to do exactly nothing. I would not be this generation's Louisa the Love-Wrecker; I would continue to be myself instead of the Mater Version 2.0 she so hoped I would morph into.

I told her I had to go, hung up over her protest, and waved my friends back to the car. As they climbed in I powered off my phone and made snarling, snapping-teeth sounds at it.

"Are you all right, Miz Xana?" DeLeon said, turning around in the driver's seat to assess the damage. He elided the letters in "all right" so that it sounded like "ah-ight."

"Peachy," I said. "Roll on, big river."

He looked at me. I nodded that I was good to go. He looked at Thorne, who looked at me and nodded at DeLeon that I really was all right.

After that we passed a long series of salt flats flanking the highway as we drove through the Great Basin Desert. After Lovelock the highway shifted northward and DeLeon said, "About an hour now."

The desert sun heated my neck and shoulders through the rear windshield and I was glad for the air conditioning.

An hour later, DeLeon pulled off the interstate onto East Winnemucca Boulevard and drove a few blocks, parking us in front of the Winnemucca Visitors and Convention Center, which, according to the lettering on the marquee, also housed the Buckaroo Hall of Fame and Wild Life Exhibits, and a big display of minerals and rocks, since mining had been the original reason for Winnemucca.

The exterior paint job on the Visitor Center was like nothing I'd ever seen; brown and green vertical striations streaking down the façade looked like water damage and moss on old barn wood. There was a palisade of short black spikes along the edge of the roof, two stories above us.

Across the street was the Sundance Casino. Before stepping through the Visitor Center's saloon doors out of the heat and into air conditioning, I scanned the block carefully for any sign of Robert Redford.

I was disappointed.

≈2 3≈

Winnemucca's population tops out at around three thousand. I was hoping that in a town that size most of the people would know each other, or at least know of each other, so the Visitor Center was, to my mind, a reasonable place to start asking for likely referrals.

"Action is eloquence," I muttered as we walked into the lobby. I hoped action would also prove to be informative.

At the main counter a petite woman sporting a bouffant dyed-black hairdo carefully sprayed into curved layers looked expectantly at the three very different people walking toward her. She was draped with a lot of silver and turquoise jewelry: cuffs, rings, squash blossom necklace, earrings, concho belt, plus matching turquoise eye shadow and broad slashes of black eyeliner. The skin on her arms was the color and texture of old parchment, but the skin of her face was a mask of foundation and blusher, settled into dry seams.

"Welcome to Winnemucca," she said. "How may I help you all?"

Her white plastic clip-on name tag showed "Shirley," next to an image of a cowboy on a bucking bronco.

DeLeon and Thorne tipped their heads at me, indicating this was my show.

"How do you do, ma'am," I said. "My name is Alexandra Bard, and I'm looking for someone who might have spoken to my father, Josiah Bard, about gold. My Dad would have been here in town maybe seven or eight years ago. I know that's a long time, so I'm hoping you would have a recommendation for where to start, knowing the area and the people like you do. Maybe there's someone who knows a lot of the history of gold mining here? That's what my Dad would have been asking about at the time. I'd appreciate any help you might be able to provide."

She smiled and tilted her head a little to the side, examining the three of us one by one. She spent the bulk of her examination on Thorne, the way women tend to do. Nodding, she turned to the door on the wall behind the counter, opened it and called out, "Elmer?"

Elmer apparently approached her, but not to where we could see him behind the wall, and Shirley covered her mouth and whispered. She peered at us, whispered some more, and laughed a little while she covered her mouth. She nodded, shut the door on the invisible Elmer, and turned back to us.

"You want to see Pete Agostino," she said. "He's been the one we send the gold fever cases to, and he has been for as long as I can remember. If your Daddy came into town asking about gold, my bet is he wound up talking to Pete at some point. I can't promise Pete'll remember anything, given that he's elderly, but you could give him a try."

"I will, thanks. Do you have a directory where I could look up his phone number? Or do you by any chance have his address?"

"Oh, he's easy enough to find." She pointed out the door. "You want to head three-four blocks down on Bridge Street here, that runs alongside this building? You go south down to Railroad. Turn right on Railroad and the bar is right there, the Mother Lode. It's a white building with a pick and shovel over the doorway. Ask anybody in there for Pete."

She smiled and nodded. There was something about the smile that I thought was off, but I thanked her as if there weren't and we turned and walked out into the blast-furnace heat.

"Somethin' about how she came up with that guy's name..." DeLeon said, looking up at Thorne.

"Recon first," Thorne said.

"I agree," I said. "That was strange. I get the feeling we're the latest patsies to be handed off to the unfriendly natives. Sending out-of-towners to

Pete is probably something everyone who lives here gets a big chuckle out of."

"But that don't mean your Daddy didn't get sent to this same joker," DeLeon said.

Rather than walk in the skin-frying sunshine, we climbed back into the now stifling car and drove, parking in the near-empty lot next to the white building at the corner of Bridge and Railroad Streets. There were motorcycles leaning on their kickstands in front of the bar, big black Harleys tricked out with leather saddle bags and passenger pillions and high-arched windshields and a lot of chrome trim.

Thorne climbed out of the passenger seat and waved at us to stay put while he did the reconnoitering. He disappeared around the front of the building.

I am trained in Krav Maga, the Israeli martial art, and I believe I am better equipped to take care of myself than many people. DeLeon is not small, and he heaves luggage into and out of his Escalade all day, which makes for extra musculature high and low on his six-foot frame. Between the two of us I thought we posed a capable pairing if faced with the possibility of a physical altercation.

Nuts to that. I let Thorne go in there on his own. Facing down heavies in a biker bar was his strong suit, and I let him deal those particular cards.

He was gone for five minutes or so, and I was wondering whether I should do something more than sit on my ass in a very toasty car, when he appeared at the corner of the building and waved for us to come ahead. DeLeon pointed at himself, wondering if Thorne meant him too, and Thorne nodded. Shaking his head, DeLeon climbed out of the car and we walked across the cracked and gravelly asphalt to where Thorne stood.

"So this guy Pete is in there?" I said.

"Yes."

"And he'll talk to me?"

Thorne nodded.

"Is it going to be safe for DeLeon?"

Because even though he's a grown man and can make his own decisions, it takes a special kind of cruel fool to invite an African-American into a white supremacist bar, which this place gave every indication of being. The place looked big enough to have pool tables in the rear of the room, and pool cues. Lots of pool cues. I'd learned stick fighting along with the Krav Maga, but I didn't know if DeLeon had taken the same training. I thought of the Five of Wands card in my café reading, with its image of men fighting each other wielding long wooden sticks.

"No problem," Thorne said.

"All right then, let's go," I said. I turned to DeLeon and put my hand on his sleeve. "If you'd rather not, I get it."

"Wouldn't miss it, Miz X. Always wanted to be a cowboy. Got the boots and all."

I looked down at his black cowboy boots with

the white tooling. He was wearing black jeans to-day instead of his black work suit and tie, but the boots were a day-to-day constant.

"Well, then, saddle up, my posse. Let's see what we can see."

The building was painted white, with no sign on the front announcing the name of the bar, just a crossed pickaxe and shovel above the wooden front door. We couldn't see much once we got inside, but at least it was cooler. The windows were curtained and our eyes took a moment to adjust in the dimness that is so popular in dive bars. There were peanut shells scattered across the painted plywood floor, and I could smell stale beer and sweat. Toby Keith was singing through the speakers in the back by the pool tables.

When we could see where we were going, Thorne led the way through the mostly empty room to the last booth along the wall opposite the bar.

An aluminum walker was folded up, leaning against the aisle side of the booth. His hand grip-ping a Budweiser bottle, a shrunken-looking man who appeared to be at least eighty years old sat at the back on the dark blue leatherette seat. He was wearing a black ball cap with "6th Army" and "Alamo Force" embroidered on the crown. Under a grimy brown suede vest (and in spite of the heat outdoors) he wore a long-sleeved tan yoke-front shirt with snap closings.

I got the impression Pete felt a chill anywhere

that didn't offer steam-cabinet warmth.

"Hello," I said. "Mr. Agostino, I'm Xana Bard."

I reached across the booth's table to shake hands and, without standing, Pete lifted a crepe-skinned hand that barely gripped mine. His cuff hung half-filled off his bony wrist.

I introduced Thorne and DeLeon and they shook hands as well. Thorne and DeLeon then turned and stood, my sentries angling themselves to face out toward the room's rear and front. I hunkered at the front edge of the table so that I would be at Pete's eye level while I spoke.

"I'm hoping you'll let me buy you another beer in exchange for answering a few questions about a man you might have met a while back. I'm told you're the local expert, and I think my father may have talked to you some years ago."

Pete Agostino looked at me, an appraisal happening behind his brown eyes, the lower lids sagging, the upper lids with a hint of epicanthic fold.

"You're Alexandra," he said, his voice an old man's tenor gargle that made me want to clear my throat. "Josh told me you'd show up, and you're just as pretty as he said you'd be. But if you're here, that means he must be dead, and you have my sympathy. He was a good man, Josh Bard was. Anyway, I was about to give up hope, waiting on you. Why don't you take a load off, young lady, and we'll have a little pow-wow."

≈24≈

Well, that stopped me. Thorne and DeLeon both turned to look at Pete.

"The MPs can sit too, if they want," Pete said, waving at my companions, who certainly carried themselves like military police. We all slid into the booth, me first in order to sit next to Pete. Closer to him, I smelled unwashed body.

"First things first," Pete said, smiling at each of us. "What's your poison, folks? Now that the gang's all here, we should maybe have a drink in memory of Josh Bard."

Thorne gestured at the Budweiser and Pete nodded, communicating in that nonverbal eye-contact-and-hand-sign way men like to do. I nodded as well, and so did DeLeon. Thorne stood up to get the bartender working on the order.

DeLeon on his own time orders Courvoisier,

but he considered himself on-duty, so the beer was going to be camouflage. I don't drink, but we were having beers here in honor of my Dad, so I'd nodded that Thorne should order me a beer. I can stare at a beer bottle as well as the next person.

"Mr. Agostino, I'm guessing there's quite a story," I said. "I'd love to hear it."

"Wouldn't you just," Pete said, not making it a question. "Call me Pete, as long as you're buying. Well, you're right, young lady, but there's gonna be some shaggy dogs along the way, and the story's gonna cost you more than one beer by the time we're done."

"Sounds like a deal."

Thorne brought back four opened long-necks. No chilled mugs, no cocktail napkins or coasters, no dish of peanuts in the shell, just beer. He put the bottles down on the table and sat, turning to face the room, ignoring his beer.

Pete tipped up his existing bottle to finish the last of it. Putting it down and pushing it to the middle of the table, he pulled a fresh one over. DeLeon handed one of the fresh bottles to me and took his own. Like Thorne, he left his sitting and turned to face the room.

"To Josh," Pete said, touching the body of his bottle to mine and taking a swig. I lifted my bottle in agreement and touched the rim to my mouth, putting it back down without actually tasting any beer. Of all the things I don't drink, beer is my least favorite. I could honor my Dad's memory without sucking down carbonated bitterness.

We sat for a moment. I was being silent, waiting for Pete to begin, letting the silence do the questioning for me. Pete had a story to tell, and he'd waited a long time to tell it, and he looked like he was raring to go.

"I was there. The Philippines liberation," he said.

"Oh? You mean in nineteen forty-three?"

I hadn't expected the story to start with the Second World War. But it was Pete's story, and he was going to tell it the way he wanted to.

"Sixth Army. Under General Krueger. He was born a Kraut, you know. A Prussian. But he wound up in the U.S. Army. He fought in the Philippines during the Spanish-American War, and against the country he was born in during World War One. He figured he was mothballed during World War Two, but MacArthur pulled him back into the field when the big push to regain those 7,000 islands was about to start. Mac-Arthur decided Krueger was familiar with the territory—never mind it'd been forty years since Kreuger'd set eyes on any of it."

"I see," I said, in what I hoped was an encouraging way.

I like history well enough, and the bar was air-conditioned, and we'd come all this way. Not only that, but Pete knew my father's and my names, and I'd spent the last eight hours mostly in a car looking at the non-scenery that is the bulk of the Silver State. I figured we'd get someplace relevant at some point. If not, at least there was cold beer to not drink.

"I was in high school in San Francisco. Balboa High. My Momma was from Tacloban, on Leyte. My Daddy was an American, in the navy, stationed at Subic Bay. Momma went up there to the base to try and get a job, because there wasn't no work where she was from, and everybody was starving, living in poverty like you wouldn't believe. She got a job working in the laundry. He married her when she got knocked up. I give him credit for that. Not many sailors would've treated her right that way."

"And after the war she moved back to the States with your father?" I said.

"And had to deal with the bullshit, pardon my French, that you had to deal with back in the Thirties, and still have to deal with, if you're not white and you marry somebody white."

"I'm guessing you dealt with the same bullshit."

He looked at me and nodded.

"I was taller than the other Filipino kids in my high school, and they all ragged me and so did the white kids. I didn't fit in with either crowd. Momma took me and my little brother over to Tacloban a coupla times to her family, and I'd grown up speaking the language at home, so I got along okay while we were there. We weren't the only half-white kids. Daddy sent Momma's family money every month, but when we visited I saw how poor everybody was, dirt poor, even with what we sent them. And when we weren't there they wrote us about how bad the Japs were, and that they were afraid of an invasion. Lord knows they were right to be afraid. When the Japs over-ran the country it was even worse than anything they'd been scared of, because the *Kempeitai* came with the army."

"*Kempeitai?*"

"The Jap secret police. But more than just po-lice. They had a unit, Unit 731, that did human experiments and all kinda biological and chemical tests. They made that Nazi Dr. Mengele look like Saint Francis. Unit 731 was mostly in northern China torturing and killing folks, but another unit of those sons of bitches, pardon my French, showed up in Leyte. We Filipinos were all *gaijin* to the Japs, so whatever they did to us was hunky-dory by their lights."

"Your Filipino family?"

Pete sniffed back the moisture that had pooled in his eyes and nodded.

"Gone," he said. "From what I can tell they got rounded up into slave labor, and either they starved to death or they got shot when they couldn't work no more."

"I'm so sorry, sir."

He sighed, took a drink of beer, and put the bottle down.

"You don't have to call me 'sir'. I was a T/3, a

Technician, which is like a corporal. But anyway, when I turned sixteen I heard on the radio that the battle of Midway had put the Japs on the run, so I lied about my age, told the recruiter I spoke Tagalog and wanted to be part of the liberation, and they took me. After Basic they sent me to be a translator on General Krueger's staff."

"So you went back to the Philippines."

"Yup. Not to Leyte, though, where my Mom's people was from. Kreuger's troops, we wound up driving the last of the Japs north off of Luzon. We chased General Yamashita's army off that island, but it was hard going, especially when we got to the Sierra Madre, with the steep terrain and the caves, and the Japs having the high ground."

I was facing Pete, my knee bent and up on the booth seat, and I saw Thorne out of the corner of my eye shift around to watch us instead of the room. I looked a question at Thorne, but he had turned to make eye contact with DeLeon.

"Miz X., a word?" DeLeon said. Thorne had tacitly forwarded interruption responsibility.

I shifted my nonverbal question to DeLeon and he stood and waved at me to come out of the booth. Thorne switched his focus to Pete.

Looking at DeLeon, I registered the room around us. It was late afternoon now, and the bar had begun to fill up. The three pool tables in the back were in use. The players were mostly big, burly, bearded, and black-leathered in one way or another.

"Would you excuse us for a moment?" I said to Pete.

He laughed and shook his head.

"Your MP's gonna tell you I'm full of shit, pardon my French," he said. "He sees what's coming and he'll tell you to fold your tent and march outta here at double time while you still can."

"I'll be right back," I said, and slid out of the booth.

≈25≈

DeLeon took my elbow and steered me far enough away that we couldn't be overheard by Pete.

"He's right about me advisin' you to walk away," DeLeon said.

"Why?"

"Because he's gonna tell you he found Yamashita's gold."

"What? What the hell is Yamashita's gold?"

"The main thing you need to know is it's a myth. General Yamashita was supposed to have been hidin' the gold the Japanese looted from folks they conquered all over Asia and the Pacific. The story generally goes that he and his troops buried it in caves all over, particularly in the Luzon mountains, since Luzon's the island closest to Japan. When the U.S. took back the islands, they supposedly found the gold by making a secret deal with Yamashita so he'd tell them where it all was. The U.S. kept the recovery a secret, stowin' the treasure underneath Fort Knox, or maybe spreadin' it around to a bunch of big banks in Switzerland and Grand Cayman and Panama, where the bankers know to keep that news to themselves if somebody ever asks.

"In the Truman and Eisenhower days, and maybe after that, the U.S. used the gold for all these right-wing hush-hush projects that the government wouldn't have gotten congressional go-ahead for: Coups, dictatorships they installed in South America and the Middle East, the Bay of Pigs, that kinda thing. Supposed to hold off communism. These days there's books and video games about Yamashita's gold, but it's like the Loch Ness Monster or the Yeti. What I'm sayin' is, this guy's blowin' smoke."

"But he knows about my Dad. He knew our names."

"So your Daddy talked to him, the same way we're talkin' to him. He's the point man for anybody comes to town askin' about gold, just like we thought when the woman in the Visitor Center sent us along here. It's how the folks in Winnemucca honor his service in World War Two, is my guess. Everybody here sends folks to him so the suckers can buy him beers and he can tell this same story over and over again. If he really knew where Yamashita's gold was, do you think he'd still be sittin' in a redneck bar in Winne-fuckin'-mucca, Nevada?"

I was facing the back of the room, toward the booth where Thorne remained with Pete. Pete sipped his beer. Beyond them I saw the six or seven men at the pool tables, pool cues in hand, watching me and DeLeon.

Uh oh, I thought. *Unless we're careful we're heading into the Five of Wands card.*

"How do you know about Yamashita's gold? I've never heard of it."

"Anybody who's ever bought or sold gold, who knows anything about precious metals or investin' in those commodities, has heard about Yamashita's gold. The U.S. was supposed to have made this deal with the Japs to not hold war trials like Nuremberg in exchange for the locations of the caves. And the U.S. didn't hold trials in the Pacific, except for one guy: General Yamashita. They executed him on trumped-up charges, supposedly after he'd given up the cave maps. Word was that Yamashita'd brought all these craftsmen in from Japan, guys who did ceramics, so that even if you stumbled over the right cave, you wouldn't find the gold because it was invisible behind these undetectable false fronts."

"Why would the General give up the gold? Why wouldn't he try to keep it for Japan after the war?"

"Again, this is all a story people tell, no facts required. Yamashita thought he was savin' his fellow officers' honor by makin' a deal that would keep all of them from goin' on trial, and would let them return to Japan and resume power. Even more important, the Emperor wouldn't have to step down. Supposedly Yamashita trusted us, and supposedly we kept the deal, except with him, because after the war we didn't want him goin' back and retrievin' any of the gold he 'forgot' to tell us about, for Japan to use instead of us. There's been a cottage industry in Philippine treasure maps ever since 1945 and, big surprise, nobody's ever found so much as a nugget. What I'm sayin' to you is that whatever this guy is about to tell you, it is guaranteed to be straight outta the barnyard horseshit. For real."

I thought for a moment.

"I want to hear him out, DeLeon. I want to get to the part where he spoke to my father, and I want to find out what he told him, and what, if anything, my father said he might do next. I want to know why Pete recognized me, and how he knew I would come to see him."

DeLeon considered that, and said, "Ah-ight then. Just so you know where this is headin' and you're ready for it."

"We're headed to guaranteed horseshit-ville. Got it."

Back at the booth, my MPs stationed between the pool-cue-wielders' access to Pete and me, I watched out of the corner of my eye as the players returned to their games.

"I'm sorry for the interruption, Pete. You were telling me about how tough the fighting was in the mountains."

"Your friend warned you off, didn't he?" Pete said, taking another swallow of beer.

"He did."

"But you're back for more."

"I am."

I smiled at Pete Agostino and he smiled back at me, showing missing molars behind his canine teeth.

"Well, then, let's have another beer to celebrate," he said.

Thorne stood and headed to the bar.

"You got your MPs well trained," Pete said. DeLeon looked at him, giving him the full-on MP stink-eye.

"Pete, they are anything but," I said. "In spite of your service to this country and the guys playing pool over there, if you want to continue to enjoy your life in this booth in this bar with this beer, I suggest you get back to your story, please."

"Well aren't you just a pistol."

I nodded and smiled, accepting Pete's assertion that I am a pistol.

"Alamo Force," I pointed at his ball cap. "You were chasing General Yamashita off the island of Luzon, but the terrain made it tough going."

Thorne put a fresh beer in front of Pete and sat facing out toward the pool tables.

"Those Japs didn't give up easy, that was for

damn sure," Pete said, draining the last of his former beer and picking up the new bottle.

"Because they didn't want to give up the caves."

"Yep. I see your guard dog told you right. We didn't know why they were fighting so fierce at the time. We figured that was just the way all the Japs fought, since we heard stories about other places they hung on to down to the last man. We only found out about the gold later, when we liberated some of the slave laborers and they told us. They had to carry the loads up the mountains and into the caves. Once the gold and the rest of the treasure was sealed inside, most of the laborers got shot so they couldn't tell nobody, but some of 'em managed to slip away and survive. Skeletons, they were. Talking skeletons. I got tasked with translating what they said."

"If General Yamashita told the U.S. where all the caves were, why are people still buying treasure maps and wandering around the cordillera on Luzon looking for it?"

"Because General Yamashita didn't tell the U.S. everything. He held some locations back."

"And you know this how?"

"Because I was the translator for the people who carried the loot up to the caves, and General Yamashita wasn't the only one who held some of the locations back. I saw the maps because I was right there with the laborers, pointing out the cave locations for General Krueger. The laborers told me Yamashita was leaving some of the caves off the map he was giving the General. I told those poor souls that I'd help them recover the gold if they'd tell me some locations later, after the General and his officers left the map room."

Pete lifted his new beer in a general toast and sipped from the cold bottle.

"And so you went back later and found the gold that the U.S. missed."

"No."

He wagged his beer bottle back and forth to confirm his denial. I looked at him, my eyebrows raised.

"I'll bite, then. What happened to the gold that the U.S. didn't locate and commandeer?"

"You got to understand, young lady, what war is all about."

I opened my hands, inviting him to tell me.

"It ain't all neat and tidy just because the brass sign some papers and take some pictures handing each other their swords. There's holdouts who didn't get the word so they keep shooting, and there's refugees, and no food, and bodies of dead kids lying on the roadside. The cities are bombed so there's no place to live and no running water. There's no gas for transport, but the roads are all bomb-cratered so why try to drive anywhere, and the government is unstable, sometimes for years afterward. There's black markets and bribes and nobody trusts nobody else. People die after the war's over just like they do when the war's going on. Meanwhile, I was in the Army. I couldn't just up and go AWOL. If I'da done that and they'da found me, they'da shot me. So I had to bide my time."

"For how long?"

"Until after I was injured and demobbed and sent back to the States. I had to spend time at the Fort Miley VA Hospital recovering from shrapnel in my leg, and it's never been right since. Some idiot found a grenade and set it off in the marketplace where a bunch of us GIs were hanging out one day after the Japs had surrendered. And then once I was mostly healed up it's not like I could fly back to Manila, wander up the mountains into a cave, fill up a backpack, and sashay out of the country with a stash of gold bricks. How'm I gonna transport it anywhere? Gold is heavy as hell. You can't take it through Customs anywhere on this planet without risking a lot of questions, and most likely arrest. It's a big project, opening up those caves and pulling out all that gold on the sly. It wasn't just coins or bars. It was statues and jewelry and gemstones and ornaments, some of them pretty large. It takes planning and resources and payoffs."

"And?"

"Have you ever heard of Ramon Magsaysay?"

"No."

"Of course not. He started out as a mechanic, but after the Japs invaded he wound up alongside that corn-cob-pipe-chewin' son of a bitch MacArthur, pardon my French. Ramon was almost chased off the island at Bataan, but he slipped away and kept up the fight from the mountains until the war was over. Big hero. After the war he went into politics, and he came here to the States to argue for veterans' benefits for his Filipino guerillas, which he got, believe it or not. During that visit I met him at the VA Hospital. Magsaysay wound up being president of the Philippines not much later."

"I hear a collaboration coming."

Pete nodded. "He had the power and I had the information."

"You say he fought in the mountains."

"Magsaysay's men had been all over the Luzon Sierras while the Japs were burying the gold, and the U.S. had to hurry to dig up everything before Magsaysay's people could find it. My advantage was I'd spoken to the laborers, some of whom died pretty quick because they were in such bad shape, and their knowledge died with 'em. But I had a copy of the map, and I was sure I knew where some of that gold was that the U.S. didn't know about, and Magsaysay didn't know about either. He and I, we made a deal. I just had to be sure I could get my share of the gold and get back to the States in one piece. I mean, he was pretty good as Filipino presidents go, in terms of there not being too much corruption while he was in charge. They called his term the 'golden years,' can you believe that? But it was a stalemate for eight years because we didn't trust each other, so the deal never worked out. And then he died in a plane crash in fifty-seven, four years before his term was up. Or maybe his plane was made to crash."

"Whoa."

"Yeah. 'Whoa' is right. And then time went on and I had no family left over there, and my Momma passed, and then my Daddy, and I had this bad leg and no money, so I didn't know how to get things moving again, and then along came Rogelio Roxas and Ferdinand Marcos.

"Ferdinand and Imelda of the ten thousand pairs of shoes."

"Those fuckin' shoes, pardon my French."

"Who was the other man you mentioned?"

"Rogelio Roxas. He found one of the caves. Turned out his father was one of the laborers I talked to after the liberation."

"So you were too late?"

"For that cave, yeah. But Rogelio had no joy of finding it. He tried to sell a gold Buddha and some gold coins and Marcos came after him, had him arrested and beaten up, and took all the treasure. After the Marcos regime fell, Imelda said Yamashita's gold had been the basis of their fortune, but other folks said the Marcoses were just a couple of kleptocrats and Yamashita's gold didn't figure into it."

Pete shook his head and took another pull on his beer before continuing.

"Believe what you want. But Ferdinand was a cagy old guy, vicious as a mongoose. I sure didn't want him for an enemy. He managed to hang on after he had Benny Aquino assassinated, and after he imposed martial law, and even after his kidneys failed, until 1986. I couldn't see myself coming out on the safe side of any deal with Marcos after what happened to Roxas."

"Pete, that's more than thirty years ago. I'm wondering if we could get to the part where you met my Dad?"

"I'll need another beer for that."

Thorne was on his way to his feet when I waved him back down and lined up my untouched beer, Thorne's untouched beer, and DeLeon's untouched beer in front of Pete, who smiled and nodded.

"Did Josh come here to meet you?"

"Everybody comes here to meet me."

"And?"

"I told him the same story I just told you."

I waited for more. Pete took a sip of beer.

"Pete."

"It took years. Your Daddy was a smart man. And an honest one. I wasn't expecting that."

Pete shook his head and looked down at the table. He'd downed enough beer to blur his voice and charge his tone with emotion.

"You finally recovered the gold."

"Josh did. I was too old and too lame to do the heavy lifting. I used to go dig up opals north of town here, in the old mine tailings, when I'd feel the urge to go prospecting. I found any stones, I'd sell 'em for beer money. But my leg got so bad I couldn't even do that no more."

"So you gave Dad the map and he retrieved the gold."

"We made a deal. He'd get the gold and split it with me, fifty-fifty. I was getting up there, and time was passing, and I decided I had to take the chance or forget about it altogether. Because what would I lose? If he stole all of it I wouldn't be any worse off, and if he kept his word I'd be rich at last. But lo and behold, he found some cash after I told him the story, enough to finance the job."

"When was this?"

"Oh Jeez, maybe around the time we started losing that liar's war in Eye-raq."

"So what happened?"

"Well, I told him how risky it was, and that even if he did manage to find it and get the gold out of the country, once he started to sell it people would notice and maybe chase his family down and hurt 'em if they couldn't track him and rob him of the treasure. So he held off while we talked about how to handle that."

"And you decided he should fake his death."

"We did that. He had some reason, something about nickel mining. Anyway, I knew there was a whole cottage industry set up in Manila for faking your death and setting up a new identity."

"You are joking."

"I'm not."

"But there was a car crash. There was a man in the car who burned up."

Pete looked up at me and nodded. "That was Harry." He looked back down at his beer.

I put my face in my hands. "Pete. Seriously."

"I admit, if I take a step back and look at all this, it's got all the earmarks of a complete cluster-fuck, pardon my French."

"Pete." I looked back up at him and shook my head, "it's not swear words I'm worried about here. It's murder. My father was just murdered. Now you're telling me some guy named Harry was murdered as well."

"No, that ain't it at all." Pete wagged his index finger in denial of Harry's murder. "Harry Lamirato was his name, and he volunteered. He had the cancer real bad, and he made a deal with Josh that his family would get money to live on."

"Oh well, then. That makes it perfectly legiti-mate."

My speaking volume had gone up. Thorne and DeLeon were on their feet, facing the pool players, who were standing in a row staring at our booth, pool cues held across their bodies.

I caught myself, put up both hands in a "Hold on" gesture to the pool players, and turned back to Pete. I felt the upholstery lift under me when DeLeon and Thorne sat back down. Pool balls clacked as the players resumed their games.

Something had altered in Pete's demeanor

once we began dealing with more recent times. He kept staring at the beer bottles, drinking faster to finish them all up. I thought he seemed ashamed, and he wanted to be drunk enough that he wouldn't feel the shame so acutely.

"Pete, if my Dad recovered the gold, then where is it now? And why don't you have your share? Because my father would have kept his word to you."

Pete hung his head for a few seconds before looking at me and answering.

"I know that. But I spent so many years hedging my bets and watching out for double-crosses that I lost the habit of believing that some people are straight. I couldn't get that gold myself and I couldn't see how anybody else would get it and then give some of it up. Gold does something to your mind."

"What did you do?" I had lowered my voice; I was almost whispering. I put my hand gently on Pete's forearm.

"I hedged my bet," he said. "I planned on a double-cross. When I realized Josh was gonna come through with my share, it was too late." He shook his head and stared at his beer. "I don't want to talk about it no more."

I asked Pete a lot of questions anyway: Who was Harry Lamirato and how did he get connected with my Dad's disappearance? Who did my Dad get the expedition money from, since Bix had only lent him five thousand dollars? When had Dad gone to the Philippines and when had he returned? Did Dad really recover the gold? Where had he been and what had he been doing in the intervening years? Why, when I saw him two weeks ago, was he an unrecognizable homeless-looking person? And then, when I found him dead, how had he become a cleaned-up but thinner, tanner version of his former self?

In the middle of the frustrating interrogation without a lot of answers Pete excused himself, pointing at the empties in front of him and then at the hallway with "Restrooms" lettered above the doorway. He unfolded his walker and limped unsteadily past the pool tables.

"He's goin' for the back door," DeLeon said, watching Pete disappear down the hallway. "You want to stop him?"

"I do. I don't know what I've got, or what to do with it."

"Outside," said Thorne.

We started to follow Pete, but the pool players lined up in a phalanx blocking our way. We reversed direction and went out the front door instead, Thorne facing the men behind me and DeLeon leading the way in front of me.

"Is there going to be a fight if we try to stop him?" I said.

"You bet," said Thorne.

≈26≈

Out in the parking lot the high desert dusk
brought with it welcome cooler air. We walked
alongside the building toward the rear, the three
of us spreading out among the parked cars and
listening for anything alarming.

Thorne walked away from the building to
gain an angled sightline to the back door. DeLeon
stayed back so he could watch the front door, in
case Pete tried to fool us that way. I stopped, hiding behind a pickup truck cab waiting for instructions, since it's still on my "Oh hell no" bucket list
to get into a biker bar fight. I thought Thorne and
DeLeon might have more experience in this arena
than I did.

Thorne has made it clear to me that avoiding a
fight is always smarter than having a fight, so I
was ready to be as smart as possible. Action that

involves being thwacked with a pool cue is not eloquent, in my view; it falls into the preposterous chaos category.

Thorne looked everywhere, the way he does, and beckoned me over to him. He pointed at the Chrysler and made a turn-the-key motion, and DeLeon backed away, aimed the key fob to unlock the car, climbed in, started the engine, and pulled out of the parking slot so we could get the doors open easily.

I suppose Pete really did have to take a piss, given the half dozen beers I saw him drink, because it was a few minutes before the back door opened and he shuffled out past a blue dumpster, leaning on the rails of his walker. Half a dozen pool players accompanied him holding their cue sticks and forming a wall around him. I could see knife sheaths on their belts and was glad the knives weren't out yet.

Thorne tapped my shoulder, indicating I should do something, probably talk, the way I so like to do and he doesn't.

"Pete," I called, stepping out from behind the truck so Pete could see me without Thorne or DeLeon. "I just want to know where my Dad went to next, please. After you and he made the deal. I don't hold you responsible for anything. But Pete, three days ago somebody stabbed him in the back and left him in my yard. Someone wanted me to find him there when I came home. I can't just let that go."

Pete and his dragons stood still. He stepped forward through their ranks so I could see him.

"Mariposa," Pete said. "The Tuolomne Mine in Mariposa." His mouth had trouble forming the complicated vowel sounds of "Tuolomne."

"Did you send him there?"

He gathered himself, finally meeting my gaze.

"I did. I knew they had the money to back the deal. But now you listen to me. They got your Daddy and they could just as easy come for me, or you, and your MPs won't stop 'em. Gold fever can make people crazier'n cockroaches after a light comes on. I owe Josh for getting that gold, even if I never seen a single piece of it. He told me he had it and was on his way. He said you'd seen him but he was too rough-looking from all the years working the mine and you didn't know him. He told me he was going to get cleaned up before he tried again and that he was going to bring the gold to me in a few days. I thought he was stalling, so I called those people down at the mine, trying to work the thing from both angles. But they kilt him first.

"Young lady, I am truly sorry. Your Daddy said you were right to give him the boot when you did, and he forgave you, so I did what I promised Josh and I told you the story. That won't square things, but it's all I can do. Now I got no more to tell you. You got to leave and don't come back, and don't tell nobody you talked to me neither."

"Mariposa," I said. "Tuolomne Mine. Thank you."

Pete nodded. I waved and turned to go to the car. Thorne followed, watching everything in every direction.

DeLeon drove gracefully out of the parking lot without leaving rubber on the broken asphalt. Leaving lots of rubber with a noise like a piglet being tortured is what I would have done.

≈27≈

The decision we mulled over was whether to stay in Winnemucca or start the drive to Mariposa right away. Mariposa is an old mining town just outside the entrance to Yosemite National Park, so the roads leading to it are well maintained in order to handle the summer tourist traffic. That meant they'd be easy enough to negotiate in the dark, and some motel offices might be open all night.

But it takes over six hours to drive from Winnemucca to Mariposa, first on the wide interstates and then on the state and county roads leading up into the foothills of the California Sierras. A more scenic drive, but one that would require at least seven hours, was the one that cut south on Route 395 in Nevada and twisted up through the California Sierras on switchback two-lane roads.

We opted for speed over scenery, dinner before driving, and sleep before Mariposa.

We ate at a decent Mexican restaurant in Winnemucca before I took the wheel and drove the two and a half hours back to Reno, where there were more hotel choices. At the hotel I called home and learned that nothing new had happened. Everyone, including dogs and cats, was doing fine without me.

≈28≈

After breakfast the next morning we climbed back into the car and aimed for Sacramento, where we swung south onto Highway 88 and then onto Highway 99. California 99 is a multi-lane highway, but it's also the old truck route linking the string of San Joaquin Valley farming towns, so the road bed was often chewed up by the eighteen-wheelers. The Chrysler handled the ride quietly and smoothly, as usual.

DeLeon was put in charge of our musical entertainment for the day, and we listened to Dr. Lonnie Smith, Chester Thompson, Faye Carol, Michael O'Neill, and Kenny Washington. We were quiet, listening to the music as we drove past French Camp, Lodi, Stockton, Manteca, Modesto, Turlock.

By the time we left the highway at Merced to

fuel up and get some lunch at a coffee shop, I had formulated a plan, and it called for action, if not terribly eloquent action.

The plan consisted of:

1.   Go to the Tuolomne Mine.
2.   Ask questions.
3.   Avoid getting killed.

Eating my BLT on toasted wheat with sweet potato fries, I was proud of the plan as I laid out the three specifics on the task list. DeLeon and Thorne bit into their cheeseburgers while I spoke.

DeLeon swallowed and said, "I think step three needs to move up in priority."

"Seconded," Thorne said.

"Passed unanimously," I said. "'Avoid getting killed' is now the first step of the plan."

While Thorne was paying the check at the cash register and DeLeon and I were standing by the door, I flashed back to the cards I'd seen at the reading in the East-West Café.

"The cards were more about my Dad than they were about me," I said.

"What cards now?" DeLeon said.

"The ones from the other night at the café."

We walked to the car as I kept talking.

"I looked at the layout and attributed all the disputing and self-generated widowhood to my siblings and me. That's not it. The fighting centered around the Emperor Card, and I think that card mostly relates to my father. I think you were right, DeLeon, when you said the Queen of

Wands card was me, and I was outside the rest of the cards watching. I mean, I'm in the reading too, but my worry that my brothers and sisters would wind up fighting and that the family would fracture—so far I think that worry is unfounded, because the four of us are getting along really well. I think the fracture was when we banished Dad all those years ago, and the fighting in the card layout is what happened all around him and to him because of this gold adventure he went off on."

Thorne and DeLeon waited while I talked myself out. They're smart that way. When they saw I was finished DeLeon unlocked the car and we got in for the last leg of the drive to Mariposa. There was more information up there, and I would find it out, and with the aid of my MPs we'd all get back out of town unkilled.

≈2 9≈

Mariposa is pretty much a Main Street sort of town, with California Highway 49, named for the Gold Rush year, as Main Street. Mariposa acts as the entry point to the Yosemite Valley, and tourists eat there and fuel up their cars and RVs, many choosing to stay in a local motel rather than camp in the park or pay the exorbitant hotel prices inside the gates.

Google did not know anything about a business named "Tuolomne Mine," so we were going to have to rely once again upon the kindness of strangers. The Sugar Pine Café looked likely, so we parked, climbed out into the dry heat and hard blue sky, and found an empty booth in the cool and mostly empty restaurant.

It was too early for dinner, so we all had iced tea and the men ordered pie. When the waitress, whose name tag read "Laney," delivered the check I asked her where the best place to start would be if I wanted to find a local mine.

"Which one? All the old ones are mined out and shut down."

"Tuolomne Mine is the name I know."

"You want Olivia Marcotte," she said. "She usually comes in for dinner at around six."

"Well, that was easy."

"Listen, there aren't a lot of jobs here. Somebody with more money than sense decided the Tuolomne might still have some gold, just down below where it's been mined so far. When permits get issued that might lead to some jobs down the line, people talk. The idea that the Tuolumne might reopen caused a lot of gossip, but so far there's only jobs for the crew doing the sampling. Olivia's the geologist and Allan Wolf is the site manager. They're kinda regulars here, but if they're not here for dinner they're likely at the Charles."

She pointed across the street to another restaurant.

"Did a man named Bard ever come in? Tall, sixtyish, blond hair going gray, blue eyes? Maybe a beard?"

"Oh hon, so many folks come through, I'm sorry but I just can't remember 'em all. There's a woman who got the sampling permits issued, and she used to come in with Olivia and Allan, but she's not a regular. She still comes in by herself from time to time, but not so much that I ever learned her name."

"Do you happen to know where the mine's office is? Or the actual mine location if it's separate from the office?"

Laney explained how to get to the mine up Route 49 a few miles north of town, and I thanked her. Thorne left an oversized tip, the way he so enjoys doing, and we headed north, following the route that gold prospectors had traversed a hundred and seventy years ago, when California had only recently been wrested from Mexico.

In 1849 men with gold fever had to either cross the immense country by wagon train or sail all the way around South America to get to San Francisco. It would have taken them a day with a pack mule to travel from Mariposa to the site of the Tuolomne Mine. I was glad for the Chrysler and the air conditioning and the Hemi engine powering us swiftly up the road. Watching heat shimmer off the asphalt paving, I wondered if I would ever again be someplace that wasn't too damned hot.

As we drove, DeLeon resumed DJ duties and Miles Davis sketched Spain for us.

I've been to Spain. It's hot there.

≈30≈

Thorne looked right and I looked left as DeLeon drove us past live oaks whose leaves were faded to sage green, Indian paintbrush the color of dried blood, and bleached foxtail and wild oat grasses. Even with both of us looking we nearly missed seeing the small "Tuolomne Mine" sign on the entrance gate, and DeLeon had to continue rolling forward until he reached a straight stretch of highway where he could turn the car around.

Once back at the gate, carefully because at that point the roadway was a blind curve, we crossed the highway into a rutted gravel driveway. We passed through the open metal-bar gate bearing the much-smaller-than-expected yellow sign with green lettering.

Raising a dust cloud as we wound slowly around the perimeter of the hill, we reached the top and drove through another open gate into a level chain-link fenced area bearing a matching small sign.

A pale green building, sixty feet square, squatted to our left. We parked away from the building, backing up to the chain link fence, next to a battered white pickup truck and a dusty but new black Lexus SUV.

The building couldn't have been less glamorous; constructed of vertical aluminum siding, it sat on a concrete slab with a corrugated metal roof thirty feet above the floor. Roll-up metal doors were open on two sides, to allow whatever breeze managed to arise from the surrounding foothills to flow through and "cool" the building, whose only other method for dissipating the heat was to provide shade.

All around the building on racks were white trays separated into long narrow troughs full of gray and white and brown and black cylinders of what I learned later were test hole rock samples.

A slender short-haired woman wearing a thin long-sleeved hoodie, linen drawstring pants and hiking boots stepped outside as we opened the car doors and climbed out into the sunshine and heat. Her hood was pulled up over her hair in spite of the temperature outside. Long auburn bangs swept across her forehead.

"Can I help you?" she said, her tone neutral.

"I hope so," I said. "I'm looking for a man named Josiah Bard."

I didn't give my name and I left out the part about my Dad's death. I wanted to see what, if anything, these folks knew before the word "murder" entered into the conversation.

"Mr. Bard isn't here."

"Is he expected?"

She paused before answering. "I don't believe so. You'd have to ask the owner about that."

"Is the owner here today? Or do you have a phone number I could call?"

The woman turned and called back into the building: "Catherine?"

I felt Thorne's hand at my back. Something told him, if not me, that the show was about to start. He moved a few feet away from my side and, without exchanging words or looks with Thorne, DeLeon moved away in the other direction. I've learned that they do this so we form three separate targets.

A trim short-haired brunette, just over five feet tall, stepped out of the building. She wore a tan polo shirt and khaki cargo pants tucked into desert boots the color of dead leaves. The sun glinted off a thick gold bangle bracelet and gold hoop earrings. I saw a gold band on the ring finger of her left hand, the one she held to her forehead to shield her eyes from the sun's glare.

"Yes?" she said. I walked, crunching across the gravel toward her, so we wouldn't have to raise our voices to talk.

"Hello," I said, standing ten feet away from

her and the hooded woman. I decided to add more information since she was the mine owner. "My name is Alexandra Bard, and I'm trying to find my father, Josiah Bard. I was told he came here. It may have been some time ago."

I saw Catherine's face shift, and the hooded woman turned to look at her, putting hands on hips as if she were making some sort of point.

Catherine looked Thorne up and down, did the same to DeLeon, and then looked back at me. She reminded me of a cat staring at a bird outside her window: eager, focused, lethal, thwarted.

"You should come in out of the heat," she said. "I ought to be hospitable, since you're my stepdaughter. The outriders can come in too, if they like."

"Excuse me?" I thought perhaps I hadn't moved close enough to hear her clearly. "Step-daughter?"

"That's right, dearie. I'm Mrs. Josiah Bard."

≈31≈

The woman who claimed to be my stepmother lowered her hand to beckon me into the building. The hooded woman she introduced as Olivia Marcotte followed her. So did I, and so did Thorne and DeLeon, out of the hot blue day into the welcome gray shade of the concrete and metal building.

A wood-frame balcony ran around three sides of the interior. Stacked cardboard boxes and racked three-inch metal pipes were stored on the balcony. Across the room was a partition with a door that bore a sign saying "Rest Room."

A heavyset bearded man stood in front of that partition, staring at a large sheet of paper spread out on a plywood plank table, chunks of gray rock holding down the corners the paper. I waved hello to him and he nodded back.

"That's Allan, the site manager," Catherine

said. "Olivia here is our geological technician."

Catherine led us through a doorway into an office created out of two-by-fours and wallboard under the balcony. We passed a stand hung with a sheaf of topographic maps that were wild with color: pink, orange, yellow, turquoise, leaf bud and bottle green, lavender, indigo.

Olivia dragged in and unfolded metal chairs and set them up. Catherine waved at them, inviting us to sit. We sat, and Olivia left us. I imagine she would have shut the door behind her to allow us privacy if there had been a door to shut.

Reaching into a mini-fridge beside her, Catherine pulled out three pint-sized bottled waters and handed them across the messy desktop to me. On the desk's surface were stacks of papers, cylindrical pieces of white quartz speckled black and gray, colored pencils, a thick bound book with blue cardboard covers and paper-clipped interior pages. A dark metal hollow cylinder with inch-wide flat grooved teeth around the upper opening acted as a pencil holder. An unruly cluster of pens, pencils, letter openers, and scissors jutted out of the teeth. Something sparkled in the teeth as I leaned forward to take the waters and hand them to Thorne and DeLeon.

"Thank you," I said.

"You're welcome." She smiled, or I suppose it was more like a smirk. "I assume you're surprised. Josiah told me you and he were estranged, so I don't suppose you knew."

"I did not."

The smirk settled in. She enjoyed having the advantage of surprise, or maybe the smirk was a permanent fixture.

I felt Thorne's arm stretch behind the back of my chair. He'd leaned back and crossed his legs, as if he was seeking a way to relax his massive body on the too-small folding chair. He didn't grip my shoulder or press his hand against me as if I needed his support. He was just there, letting me know he was there.

"Your father said you had a nickname. Should I call you Xana?" She pronounced it "Zana."

"Alexandra is fine," I said.

I felt somehow that allowing her to call me "Xana" would give her power, like the straw-weaving princess gained power over the dwarf by calling him "Rumpelstiltskin." I didn't think I would fly into a rage and disappear if she said my name, but I didn't like the intimacy of her using it.

I thought of the Emperor card, and its attribution of power and control and authority, and my intuition told me this woman would do her best to dominate the situation, starting with using my "secret" name.

To divert her attention from the name rebuff, I introduced Thorne and DeLeon, and the men nodded but did not reach to shake hands with her, nor did she reach out to them.

I looked more carefully at Catherine now that we were inside, out of the blinding sunshine. She was attractive, but past the bloom of pre-menopausal women. Crows' feet fanned out from her eyes and there was loosened skin at her jawline. A permanent groove ran from the sides of her nose to the corners of her full, wide lips, and there were frown lines etched at the inner edges of her eyebrows. Ropy veins on the backs of her hands stood out amid age spots that were faint but unmistakable. She didn't dye her straight bobbed hair, and gray filaments muted the intensity of the original dark brown. When she spoke I could see perfectly straight, white little teeth, sharp like a ferret's.

"I'd like to know the story of how you met," I said.

I kept the request simple. Most people like to tell their story, and Catherine proved to be no different. But first I had to answer her qualifying questions.

"Do you know where Josiah is?" she said.

"I do."

"And where is that?"

"He passed away in San Francisco earlier this week. I'm sorry."

Again, I kept it simple. I hadn't liked the smirk. I watched in vain for surprise or grief-strickenness.

"Ah," was what she said. She thought for a moment, looking down at the desk. She picked up a brown pencil with a yellow lead and tapped it a few times against the desktop.

"Well, I'm very sorry to hear that," she said.

"We all were."

I noticed she didn't ask how he died. But Mariposa isn't Mars; people there can find out what's happening in the world, including murders in San Francisco, and perhaps the news had already reached her.

"Had you two reestablished contact?" she said.

"No."

"Do you know if he spoke with anyone in the family before he passed away?"

"He did not."

We were silent again. I was waiting, and she was thinking.

"He was an extraordinary man," she finally said, looking me in the eye as if daring me to disagree.

"Yes, he was."

"To answer your question, Josh and I met through my brother, Jeremy. I believe you know him."

"McDunnigan?"

"Exactly. They worked together at the bank, before Josh left."

Well, that explained why she wasn't surprised to hear that my father was dead. No doubt Jeremy had called her after he and I met up at Tadich.

She was being circumspect in her description of what had led to Dad's departure from the bank, so I did my best to match her.

"When was it, that you and my Dad first met?"

"Oh, it was prior to his leaving the bank, actually. We met at some social function. We were both married to other people back then. We met again up here, after we were both divorced, and not long after that we got married."

I didn't hear hearts and flowers in that explanation, but second marriages tend to be a more practical experience for people who've sprung for a big extravaganza on their first nuptials.

"How did he come to be up here?" I said.

She thought about what to say. I waited.

"He was looking for financial backing for a project of his. He knew Jeremy had bought this mine and was marshalling investors to fund new exploratory drilling. Josh was curious about the mine, and wondered whether those same investors would be interested in his project, since the goals were similar."

I nodded encouragingly.

"Jeremy and I often work together on projects like this. I'm a chief geologist, so Jeremy's mine investors often look to the two of us for advice. But Jeremy didn't refer Josh to me. Some odd old veteran sent him here, by pure coincidence."

She stopped and looked at me, tilting her head and assessing.

"A happy coincidence," I said.

People who need to wield power enjoy admiration a lot more than the rest of us do. Not to go all Marxian, but emperors wear robes and crowns and carry jeweled scepters and orbs so that we poor serfs will be properly dazzled and awestruck by the way our stolen labor has translated into wealth and leisure for someone else—so that we'll keep letting the leisured wealthy steal, just so we can watch them parade around looking all glittery and well-fed.

I thought Catherine saw me as a serf. I kept my awe in check but elected to dish out admiration in the largest dose I could manage.

"Do you know anything about gold mining?" she said, before I could dish out any more admiration.

"Not the current incarnation. I know the history of the California Gold Rush, and that there were mines all along the foothills here."

She nodded. "But the gold that's reachable by antique methods has long since been mined out. That doesn't mean there isn't more gold deeper down."

"I see. Which is why you reopened this mine?"

"Precisely. You see, gold is everywhere. But over eons the geologic activity of plate tectonics and ice ages and glaciers and water formation and evaporation causes the gold to concentrate around the world in certain locations more than others. The western slope of the California Sierras is one geologic phenomenon where gold became concentrated. And gold tends to show up in conjunction with other minerals such as quartzite and serpentinite, so based on the aerial survey maps we drill samples to see if those minerals are abundant, and we assay the likely samples, and look for any visible gold as well. If we can see with the naked eye any gold in a sample, that means the concentration is very high."

"The drilled assay samples are what you have in the troughs outside," I said.

"Yes. And that's a drill bit." She pointed at the toothed pencil cup on her desk. "The bit screws onto the first pipe. As the drill spins, the bit digs the pipe into the ground and rock fills the pipe. We keep screwing on more pipe until we hit carbonite, which is when we stop. There won't be any gold below the carbonite."

"The drill bit sparkles because there are industrial diamonds in the teeth?"

"Yes. As we produce assay samples the investors send their own geologists to see what we've brought up, and they decide whether to keep on investing."

I nodded again. People like to talk about the stuff they feel knowledgeable about, so I let her talk. My only task was to hit the conversational ball back across the net from time to time, moving us gradually into the game I wanted to play. But Catherine was on a roll, no volleying required, and my game-shifting would have to wait.

"This old veteran that Josiah had run into knew about the reopening of the mine here because his brother owns a tacky little souvenir shop in Mariposa, and the brother's wife works in the permit department for the county. I'd worked with her to get the mine reopened and I suppose she gossiped. There's not much else to do up here. And word traveled really fast when I hired a crew to start drilling samples."

She shrugged and spread her hands out, as if to indicate that she'd explained everything so clearly that there could be no questions, unless I was an idiot.

"I see."

Well, I saw some of it. I now understood how all the players had gotten connected with each other, but why had so many years gone by? Why had my father come to this mine when his goal was to get himself to the Philippines? How did any of this play into his faked death? And wasn't Jeremy, not Catherine, the link to the investors who would fund Dad's gold quest?

"I'm not sure about the timing of all these events," I said, remembering that I'd played the idiot with Jeremy so I should probably do the same with his sister.

"This particular mine has been a stop-and-start effort," she said. "It's been very frustrating. We purchased it almost twenty years ago, after completing the aerial survey that identifies sub-surface minerals, and then we had to jump hurdle after hurdle. Environmental regulations changed, and we had to demonstrate compliance and file revised impact statements and get new permits. County elections replaced the players we'd been working with, and we had to forge new alliances in order to renew our permits. Investors came and went as the markets devalued and revalued gold, and as our drilling assays varied in quality. We've had to shut down and reopen multiple times."

She waved her hand as if batting away a persistent, annoying insect. People who stymied her in her pursuit of a goal were bugs.

"How frustrating for you."

"It was beyond frustrating. It was positively criminal. You'd think people would recognize the inherent value of providing gainful employment in a depressed area like this."

She had raised her voice, the volume triggered by the obstructions others placed in her way.

"Of course," I said. She was tapping the pencil again. I waited until she stopped the tapping.

"During the down periods, while we waited for permits, I vetted other projects for Jeremy. He relies on my expert opinion, since I'm the geologist in the family. Josh came here originally as a laborer. Jeremy was doing him a favor, giving him a job. Apparently Josh was finally clean and sober after some problems. Josh didn't stay for long, though. He quit and was gone for some months. Then he came back after he'd talked to that old man over in Nevada. He'd put together a proposal for his own mining project. Jeremy looked to me for my signoff on Josh's proposal."

She'd said the words "mining project" without faltering. Maybe Josh had masked his plan to recover some of Yamashita's gold from her.

I decided it was time to shift to my game, if possible.

"Did you and Dad get married up here?" I said.

She looked at me with panther eyes. Her fingers curled around the pencil. I felt my face heat up in a blush.

"It's just, I'm sad that my Dad and I weren't able to reconcile before he died," I said. "I'd like to know more about what happened. I know it's too late to make up for lost time."

I heard the shudder of emotion in my voice and realized how true my words were. Catherine tilted her head and narrowed her eyes, studying me as if my emotion were a matter for curiosity instead of the norm for a grieving daughter. A few seconds passed before I swallowed and she picked up the thread of the conversation.

"We weren't interested in a having a big to-do," she said. "We went to the courthouse and the judge married us here in town."

"Ah."

She sat forward and crossed her arms on the desktop. I felt a current of charged intelligence rolling toward me. I pulled myself out of the emotional furrow I'd slid into, ruing all the lost years with my Dad.

Here we go, I thought, and looked up at her.

"So how exactly did you know to come here looking for Josh?"

"He sent me a letter," I said, and watched Catherine react as if she'd been slapped. Her jaw fell open and she uncrossed her arms, pressing her palms into the desk so strongly that she pushed her chair backward.

"A letter. He sent you a letter."

"Yes."

"Do you have it with you?"

"No." I wasn't exactly lying. The letter was in my purse in the car.

"And he sent you here."

"Yes." Well, in a roundabout way he had.

"What else did the letter say?"

"That he loved me and my brothers and sisters. That he was sorry for the bad times."

"Nothing else?"

"Catherine, he and I didn't speak or see each other for many years. I was surprised to get anything at all from him."

I hadn't answered her question, and I hoped she wouldn't notice.

"I have a question for you," I said, to keep the focus away from my lack of an answer. "Can you think of any reason why someone would want to kill my father? Because he was murdered."

"Jeremy told me about that. And no, I have no idea why anyone would want to hurt Josh."

"Did he work up here with you for months, years, what?"

She took a moment to frame her answer.

"Initially, as I said. But ultimately, with our endorsement, he managed to obtain the funding for his project, and the project took him out of town for some time."

"For how long?"

"Oh, off and on over the course of the last few years. Maybe five or so?"

"Do you know any of the places the project took him to?"

"He could be very close-mouthed about his work." There was the smirk again.

"Did you see him at all within the last couple of weeks?" I thought I might as well ask. "It looks like he was in San Francisco for a few days before he was killed."

Her eyes narrowed and she shook her head slowly. "I heard from the old guy in Nevada that Josh was back in California, but I didn't know where he was."

She was lying, I felt certain. It was clear to me that I wouldn't get any more information from Catherine, nor was she going to get any more information out of me. I stood, and DeLeon and Thorne stood as well.

"Thank you for your time, and for the information. I wish you well with the mine," I said.

She stood and gestured toward the open doorway. As we walked out she said, "It's been nice meeting someone from Josh's first marriage. You take after him."

"So people say."

"You'll let me know about the funeral," she said, a directive rather than a request. She handed me a business card and I nodded, putting the card in my jeans pocket without glancing at it.

Catherine stopped at the shaded doorway to the building and watched us walk to the car and depart, DeLeon at the wheel, down the dusty driveway and out onto the highway. Thorne reached through the gap in the front seats and took my hand in his.

In silence we cruised back through Mariposa and turned west on the highway that would take us home.

"What'd you get from all that, Miz Xana?" DeLeon said.

I looked out the window at the sun-bleached hillsides as I spoke.

"I think she was too interested in the letter. I think my Dad stiffed her on the gold, which she was hoping would save her from having to screw around digging holes in the hillsides of Mariposa."

I thought of the Queen of Swords card from my reading, of the Queen's one hand holding a bloody sword, the other hand hanging down next to the throne holding a severed man's head.

"I think he held out on her about the gold," I said. "And I think she killed him because of it."

‹‹32››

"I recognize the truck back there," DeLeon said. "It was up at the mine."

We were on Highway 140, out of the foothills and down on the flat of the San Joaquin Valley, on the outskirts of Merced. The road stretched out behind us. Thorne and I turned to look. There was a white pickup a quarter of a mile back.

"I believe you, but how can you tell it's the same truck?" I said. "It's just a white pickup. There must be a zillion of those."

"It's got an out-of-state license plate. A turquoise one. I think that's New Mexico."

"Here," Thorne said. "We don't lead them home."

Maybe DeLeon was wrong. He seldom was, but it was dinnertime anyway. So we stopped in Merced at a diner. If the truck was just a truck, fine. If it was following us, we'd be ready to intercept the driver. Besides, we could compare notes while we ate and see if anything resembling a plan would emerge. Another plus about the delay was that we would miss the indescribably horrific traffic that bottlenecked at the Bay Bridge every morning and evening at rush hour.

We sat in a booth next to a plate glass window, and then Thorne stood again.

"Down," he said, pushing air down with his palm, the way you give a hand signal to a dog. He headed back outside, moving fast with his long stride.

I slid under the tabletop and hunkered down out of sight. DeLeon slid out of the booth and frog-walked to the last booth next to the door. People stared at him as he crouched at the last booth, out of sight of the parking lot but ready to tackle anyone coming through the door.

The restaurant had been noisy, and I could hear it grow quiet as patrons registered DeLeon's odd behavior. He was the only black man in the room, he was doing something that struck everyone as suspicious, and I was worried someone would draw a gun, so I slid out of the booth and scuttled over to join him.

"What the heck is goin' on?" the cashier said, her voice loud in the now-silent restaurant.

I looked up at her and put my hand up in a "Wait" gesture.

"Something in the parking lot," I said. "Just give us a second."

The specter of omnipresent mass shootings caused panic to build in the restaurant. I could feel fight-or-flight adrenaline taking over as chairs scraped back and people prepared to scatter.

"Everything's fine. He's got her," DeLeon said, and stood, so I stood as well. Thorne had hold of Olivia Marcotte's arm as he brought her through the door and led her to the booth.

"Everything's okay now," I said to the cashier and the room in general, and I went back to the booth. Thorne and DeLeon sat flanking Olivia, who looked small and vulnerable against the back of the booth. I sat at the front edge, next to Thorne. We were quiet until the conversations around us gradually resumed.

"And what brings you to Merced today?" I asked, using my retail clerk voice.

"I tried to catch you, but your car was going too fast."

She pushed the hood back off her head and shoved her fingers through her tangled hair.

Well, the fact that our car was speeding was a general truism about how all three of us drove, so no argument there.

"Yes, but why were you trying to catch us?"

The server, a waitress wearing a red apron, appeared.

"Have dinner with us, our treat," I said, aiming to disarm the server in case she was concerned that Olivia had been forced into joining us against her will. We gave our drink orders to the server and ignored the menus she had placed in front of us. I was confident that if we opened the menus we would see glamour shots of entrees that would look nothing like the actual food we were served.

Olivia moved to drop her hands in her lap. Thorne said, "On the table," in that bass rumble of his, and she stared at him. She put her forearms back on the tabletop and clasped and unclasped her hands.

The waitress put down our drinks and held up her order pad and pen. We all opted for cheeseburgers and fries. It's the safest order in every town in every state of the country. No matter how the cook prepares a cheeseburger, it's rare to get one that tastes like a tractor tire, but if such a thing ever does happen that's why God created mustard.

"Just say it," I said.

Olivia looked at me, her eyebrows pushed into a frown, her unruly Ryan Adams-style hair flopped around her face.

"I'm a geologist. I just like rocks—have ever since I was a kid," she said.

"And?"

"I specialize in metal ores. Bauxite, galena, hematite, magnetite, all the metal oxides that you can extract and refine into elements like aluminum and iron."

"And gold."

"Yes. I get contracted all over the world to determine if a particular metal oxide is present in sufficient concentration to warrant large-scale mining. Some gold appears in nuggets and is pure without refining. But modern gold mining requires separating the gold from the surrounding rock, so the concentration has to be high enough to warrant the cost of extraction."

"Olivia, this is very interesting, but you didn't follow us to explain how gold mining works."

"You don't understand."

She continued to wring her hands and stare at the table—at anything but the three of us in the booth with her.

"What don't I understand?"

"I have to get back up to Mariposa or she'll suspect something. I told her I had to do some grocery shopping, but if I don't get back there soon she'll know I left town. She finds out everything."

She looked at Thorne and DeLeon, at their bulk blocking her into the booth.

"Then talk quickly, Olivia."

I was weary of evasions and half-truths and jockeying for position. My father had been murdered in my garden, and I could feel the truth hovering, and I would push for the truth to land kerplunk in front of us, clear and solid and strong, apparent to everyone whether they liked it or not.

The burgers arrived. Thorne and DeLeon looked to me. I waved at them to eat and picked up a fry, pointing it at Olivia for her to go on.

"They were going to salt the samples," she said.

"What do you mean?"

"Josh was supposed to bring Catherine enough gold that she could fake the assays."

"But why? The gold he found was supposed to be valuable enough in itself."

She knew about the gold Dad was supposed to recover and bring back to the U.S.; there was no need to pretend I didn't also know about it.

"She was going to double her money."

"How?"

Olivia looked at her burger and, sighing, pushed away the plate.

"Gold mining relies on a huge initial investment. Aerial surveys and mapping, drilling and earth-moving equipment, on-site buildings with power and water and cell phone service, vehicles, permits, drilling, assays, filling in all the drill holes with concrete, employee labor; it goes on and on. The mine doesn't actually make any money unless we find enough concentration of ore to make full-scale mining profitable. Our entire job up front is to justify spending money right and left. We need investors for all of it, and the odds are always against finding enough ore to ever become profitable."

"But if you fake the assays with added gold..."

"When the assays show there is enough gold to start up real production, investors come forward willingly, even though the production investment required is even bigger than the prospecting investment."

"And because the assays have been faked there's not really enough gold to make the mine profitable."

"So Catherine and her brother take the start-up money and put on a little show of opening the mine for real. After a couple of months they report to the investors how disappointed they are to conclude that the mine is in fact a bust. That the assays must have been misleading. That it's too bad, but that's the way mining goes sometimes. By then they've embezzled the investors' money, plus they have most of the gold Josh brought back. They wind up richer than God."

"But Josh didn't give Catherine the gold."

"He didn't."

"Do you know if he actually had it?"

"I don't know for sure. I think he did. But I never saw any."

"Why do you think he had it?"

"Because I heard her screaming at him. She was pissed that he was going to stick to the original agreement they made rather than allow her to cheat her investors. If I'm in the building I can hear what goes on in her office, the same way I heard you guys this afternoon."

"Which is why you followed us."

"Because I don't want to be a part of this. And I don't want anything else bad to happen, like what happened to your Dad. I didn't sign up for that, and I don't want to be associated with a mine that gets known as a fraud."

"Don't go back," Thorne said, his burger and fries eaten.

"I have to get the rest of my stuff," Olivia said.

"You don't," he said, looking down at her from his height, from his deep-set eyes to her startled ones. He shook his head. She looked at me and then at DeLeon.

"Believe him," DeLeon said. "Just eat your dinner and keep drivin'."

"Well shit," Olivia said, sighing, and pulled her plate back toward her. "Somebody give me some goddam ketchup."

≈33≈

"Well, then," Olivia said, after the waitress had taken away our dishes and we were sitting with refills on our drinks. "There are two containers."

"What kind of containers?" I said.

"Shipping containers. Like you see stacked up on big ships, or sitting at ports like Tacoma and Long Beach."

"Or Oakland," DeLeon said.

Olivia nodded. "I don't know where they are. I just heard Catherine arguing with Josh about them, because they'd arrived but he wouldn't tell her where they were or how to find them."

"Do you know who the shipper was? Or do you have a bill of lading or manifest? Do you know the port of origin? Anything?"

"I know that in just about any quantity it's mostly illegal to ship any gold that isn't finished jewelry into the U.S. I believe Josh found a way to smuggle the gold somehow. Believe me, if she knew about any paperwork identifying the shipment, Catherine would be all over it."

"That's why she was so interested in the letter Dad sent me."

"That's another reason I followed you. You told her about a letter, which means you'd better watch your back. Even if there was nothing in the letter about the shipment, she won't believe that without seeing for herself."

I flashed back to the bloody knife and the gash in my father's back.

"So let me get this straight," I said. "Somewhere in the United States, at some seaport where ships from the Philippines will dock, in a stack of essentially identical containers, there are two mystery boxes full of smuggled gold. U.S. Customs may already have confiscated the contents because raw gold is illegal to import. My job is to track down these containers before they're seized and somehow get them released to me so I can retrieve a treasure looted by Japanese conquerors more than seventy years ago. In the process of doing that, I have to avoid being killed by the same person who killed my father. But wait—there's more. The murderer *knows where I live*."

"Piece of cake," Thorne said.

"Seconded," DeLeon said.

DeLeon slowly circled his glass in the ring of condensation that had gathered under it on the

Formica tabletop. Thorne watched Olivia's hands.

"Here's the thing," Olivia said. "I liked your Dad. He was nice, he worked hard, and he didn't treat me like an underling the way Catherine does or make crude remarks like Allan does. Geologists like me go ten weeks on and then two weeks off, because the job is 24/7 while we're on, and it's tough. As of tomorrow I'm due to be off for two weeks, so I have my duffle in the truck already. I'll call Catherine and tell her I'm taking off a day early, and I just won't go back. She'll be suspicious that I'm heading out a day early, because I told her I was just going to get some groceries, but what can she do? I'm already out of there. I can be back in Santa Fe by the day after tomorrow."

"You like what you do a lot, don't you?" I said.

"Yeah. I like the independence of it. It's mostly outdoors, in all kinds of weather, in all these remote places around the world. I learn languages and eat strange food and come in contact with some amazing people. The idea of an office job gives me hives." She shuddered at the thought.

"Every couple of weeks, wherever I am," she continued, "I have to give a tour to a team of geologists coming in to look everything over in order to satisfy themselves that our samples contain what our written reports document is in there, and that we're on the up and up and deserve more investment money.

"I have a lot of friends by now in those teams.

Those friends trust me. They check everything, but they trust that what I put in the report is what they'll find when they check. When I figured out what Catherine was up to, I realized she was going to destroy my reputation. She's at the end of her career, but I'm just at the beginning of mine. Anything I can do to prevent her from trashing my reputation in a global industry, I'm going to do it."

"I'm grateful for your help. I'm just hoping you're a really successful eavesdropper as well as a reliable geologist."

Olivia thought for a few moments, staring at her Diet Coke.

"There's a hint, if you want it."

"By all means."

"You can put any number you like on your bill of lading, as long as it's not duplicating another number in the system. I heard Catherine talking about a twelve-digit bill of lading number, and that the containers had come into port on a charter instead of a regular shipping line. There's a broker handling the Customs clearances so all the inspections and approvals will go smoothly."

"If she has that information, why doesn't she have the containers?"

"Because she doesn't have that information. He showed up at the mine a couple of weeks ago while she was at the county office hassling about permits. Allan was out dealing with a pipe that was stuck in a drill hole. I told Josh how Jeremy and Catherine were planning to cheat the investors, and when she got back he told her he wouldn't be part of it. He said he'd gotten wind of the fraud elsewhere, and he kept my name out of it. I've been scouting for another consulting job since then, just hanging around because you don't give up a job until you've already got a new job."

"But if she and her brother funded Dad's project, he wouldn't have refused to repay her. I don't believe he would do that."

"He didn't," Olivia agreed. "He told her he'd reimburse her and Jeremy for the money they'd lent him, but he wouldn't give them any gold—just the money he owed plus interest. But she didn't want money; she wanted the gold so she could get the double payoff. She was yelling that commodity investors know they're taking a big risk, and that the risk sometimes doesn't pan out, and they'd just take a tax write-off so it was no big deal. When he told her it was a big deal to him and he wasn't going to give her the gold, and not only that but he was going to alert the investors to her plan, I thought she was going to kill him right then and there."

Olivia shook her head at the memory of it.

"So she had a motive, and she did see him a couple of weeks ago," I said. "She lied about that. But it's not much of a hint, that there's a twelve-digit number."

"There's also the fact that Josh chartered a ship and used a broker. With those three facts you should be able to track the containers down."

"I have to assume she's trying to do the same thing."

"But even if she finds 'em, Ms. X., it ain't like she can do anythin' about it," DeLeon said.

"She can if she's married to him and she's got a death certificate," I said.

We thought about that. It was Thorne who found the flaw in the argument.

"She told you she was Mrs. Bard," he said. "Was he Mr. Bard when he chartered the ship?"

"Do you know what name he was using?" I asked Olivia. "Because he faked his death a long time ago. I don't know how he got a new ID and a passport and credit cards in order to fly internationally, but I think he must have managed it."

"We all called him Josh, because Catherine knew him from before, from when he was at the bank with her brother. But I remember one time we had geologists visiting he was wearing a laminated clip-on name tag, and I laughed because I thought the name on there was like 'laminator' or something. Josh was The Laminator, wearing his laminated badge."

"Lamirato," Thorne said.

"Harry Lamirato?" I said.

"Could be. It's been a while."

I nodded, feeling the pieces of the puzzle continuing to fit together. I didn't know why Dad had felt the need to fake his death, though.

"Is there anything else you can tell us? Anything at all that would get us closer to why he had a new identity? Or that would help us nail down who killed him? Because we may think it was Catherine who did it, but so far there's no proof."

Olivia took a sip of her soda and put the glass down on the table.

"The wedding ring," she said.

"What about it?"

"One day Catherine wasn't wearing one, and the next day she was."

"Well, isn't that what happens? Today you're not married, and tomorrow you are and you're wearing a ring. She said it was a small ceremony at the courthouse."

"Except your father wasn't there."

"What?"

"He was gone at the time. He'd been gone for months. All of a sudden she had on a ring. She told us it was none of our business."

"Who is us?"

"Allan Wolf and me. You saw him at the mine. He's the site manager. He's also her son. She used to be Catherine Wolf."

"Does Allan know about the fraud?"

"He spends a lot more time out in the field, solving the day-to-day problems that arise, so maybe not. If he did, we never talked about it. He's kind of a quiet guy except when he's hitting on me."

"In any case, you're saying maybe Catherine isn't my stepmother after all."

"I'd ask to see a marriage license, is all I'm saying."

We were quiet. Thorne had laid money down on the check to pay the tab and extravagantly overtip. We looked at each other, silently agreeing that we were done, and slid out of the booth.

"I'm going to the cops with this," I told Olivia as we stood outside in the fading afternoon. "Will you back me up?" She thought about it, looking uphill in the direction of Mariposa.

"I will, but only about the mining fraud. I don't want to say more than that."

"That's actually perfect. Until we know for sure there is actual gold, I don't think there's any point in kicking off a treasure hunt by the police. I just want to figure out who killed my Dad."

"Sounds good," she said.

We said goodbye and traded phone numbers before Olivia drove away.

"I could take a nap," DeLeon said, so I took the wheel with Thorne in the passenger seat and DeLeon in back.

"Why would Catherine lie about that?" I said as we drove out of the parking lot.

"Which lie you mean, Miz X.?" DeLeon said. "Seem like there's a few to pick from."

"About marrying Dad."

"Community property," Thorne said.

He meant that in California a spouse has absolute rights regarding a divorcing or deceased person's assets. If Catherine had in fact managed to marry him, any gold we tracked down was half hers no matter what my father wrote in his will.

"That greed thing," DeLeon said. "So mothafuckin' reliable."

He crossed his arms, leaned back against the leather headrest, and nodded off.

⋍34⋍

Thorne and I quietly hashed out a strategy as I drove north on Highway 99 and then west at Modesto to Interstate 5. As we entered the penumbra of Bay Area civilization, I pulled off the highway for a moment and turned driving duties over to an awakened DeLeon.

From the back seat I called Walt Giapetta first, putting the call on speaker so the men could hear.

Walt answered his cell phone. It was still roughly dinnertime and it sounded like he was in a restaurant, so since he was out in public I had hopes he wouldn't start cursing and screaming at me right away.

"Walt, someone killed my Dad because he wouldn't fund a fraud," I said. "Dad had managed to obtain financial resources that he thought would be used ethically. When he found out the plan was to bilk investors, he bowed out and his bowing out killed the deal. The crooks were planning to net millions, if not more."

"Xana, what in the holy fuck do you think you're doing?" is how he felt initially about my role in his investigation. But so far he was only cursing, not yelling, which I took as a good sign.

I apologized. An apology is always a logical lead when someone's offended, although I was pretty sure an apology wasn't going to carry the day with Walt Giapetta.

"Please, Detective. I uncovered facts I don't think you could have found, nor would anyone involved have provided them to you. I also believe I've unearthed a clear lead as to who might have killed my father. I'm not going to assume you haven't also made progress. I am asking you to allow me to provide additional information that I think you will find relevant, including the motive for Dad's murder."

"I'll be at your house in ten minutes. Start praying I don't arrest you for interfering with a police investigation."

I told him I wasn't at the house and he blew another array of gaskets. I imagined him waving for a check as he threw his napkin on the table.

"Are you by chance with Mr. Thorne Ardall, the mystery tenant who refuses to return my calls?" he said.

"I'm at Altamont, headed to San Francisco right now, so I'm about an hour out."

"That's not what I asked you."

"I know."

"Ms. Bard, I want you and whoever is in that car with you to come straight to the Hall of Justice. Do not pass Go, do not collect two hundred dollars, do not go anywhere else in between. You will call me from your car when you exit the Bay Bridge and I will meet you and your passenger or passengers at the sidewalk on Bryant Street. If you do not appear within the next ninety minutes I will issue a warrant for your arrest. Is that clear?"

"Crystal," I said.

≈35≈

Between Altamont and Dublin I called Brett and told him where I was headed and why. He said he would call Nora's husband Hal for an attorney referral that he would text to me, which sounded like a good idea. I asked Brett to put Collin on the phone.

"What do you need, baby sister?"

"How good are you at research? I need somebody to track down very specific information about small chartered freighters and containers."

"Well, actually I'm splendid at research, and you have a setup upstairs that the NSC would envy. I mostly find out how explosives go kaboom and what they look like when they do their job, but tell me what you need and I'll tackle it. We're all just hanging out anyway, waiting for the funeral, so it'll give me something to do."

"Collin, this is really important, and I'll explain why later, okay? Either Dad or a guy who might be named Harry Lamirato chartered a ship, which then traveled from Asia, maybe Manila, to one of the West Coast ports, but try Oakland first."

Collin asked me to spell "Lamirato" and I did.

"Most likely it arrived in the U.S. within the last couple of weeks, with a local agent guiding two containers through Customs. Harry Lamirato or Dad shipped the two containers on the freighter, and I need to know what happened to those containers. I don't have any more than that for you to work with. If you can track down the name of the ship, a bill of lading, container numbers, anything at all more specific, that would be amazing."

"Amazingness is my special talent. For you, I will burn up the Internet and make phone calls until I'm hoarse," Collin said.

"I love you, bigger brother."

I reread the note my father had written and recited some numbers for Collin to try out when searching for the bill of lading. Then I thought about what I was asking him to do, and what the ramifications might be.

"Collin, one more thing?"

"And that would be?"

"Keep the research to yourself, please? Not a word to the sibs or to Mater. And if anybody shows up at the house, specifically a middle-aged woman announcing herself as your stepmother, don't open the door."

"Um, Xana..."

"I'll explain, I promise. But it's going to have to wait until I get home and everybody's there. Right now I'm under orders to go to the Hall of Justice and fill in the detectives on what I found out."

"Yes, yes, patience, Grasshopper. But remember, after I dig up all this information, while keeping my trap shut and barring entry to mysterious new relatives, 'Thy Thank-You Note Must Be Handwritten.'"

ה ה ה

Thorne and DeLeon pulled their suitcases from the trunk, and I left them buying fare tickets at the Dublin BART station. It would piss off Walt when I was the only one who showed up at the Hall of Justice, but there was no way for him to determine that anyone else had been driving with me, and I refused to subject either of those men to the antagonism and maybe worse that I was going to face.

I debated what I would tell Walt as the Chrysler rolled along the curves of Highway 580 where the roadway skirted the East Bay hills. I thought about Catherine and how petite she was. If she had followed Dad to my house, I wondered how she and Dad got into my garden over the six-foot fence, and then, provided she had been able to get my Dad to turn away from her so she could stab him so forcefully in the back as to kill him, how had she gotten back out of my garden?

She'd have needed the strength of Ant-Man. I couldn't see it. If she'd been involved, she'd had help.

≈ℨℴ≈

Walt and Detective DeLaRosa kept me in the homicide squad room on the fourth floor of 850 Bryant Street for long enough that I lost track of how late it had gotten.

I kept it simple: Catherine McDunnigan, now calling herself Bard, had schemed to defraud mining investors by faking mining assays with the help of her brother Jeremy, my father's former colleague at Franciscan Frères. My father had found out and threatened to blow the whistle on them. I threw in the possibility that Catherine's claimed marriage to my Dad might also be false.

I stuck to the story that money was at stake, not gold, since so far there was no actual gold, and apparently gold makes some people crazy and others incredulous. I was sure Catherine and Jeremy, if questioned, would never mention it.

I left out Harry Lamirato and his volunteered corpse. That could wait until I learned whether Lamirato was the name used for the ship charter.

I asked Walt if the autopsy and forensics had explained how my Dad wound up in my yard. I told him I couldn't understand how he'd gotten over the fence, and wondered whether the evidence showed that there had been someone else in the garden with him when he was stabbed.

Walt and Detective DeLaRosa shared a good laugh, complimented me on my chutzpah, and didn't answer my questions. When they demanded to know how I came by my information and conclusions, I shook my head and told them to verify the answers for themselves. I gave Walt Olivia's phone number for corroboration.

There really wasn't anything the detectives could do but ask me the same questions over and over, which they did, while I gave them the same answers over and over, which I did, until it occurred to me that they were messing with me because I had involved myself in their investigation. I'm sure they were also repeating the questions because they knew I wasn't telling them the whole story, plus Walt was making me pay for not bringing him Thorne. Fair enough.

I finally asked if I was under arrest, and if not I was going home. It was after midnight when I left, praying that no one had towed or vandalized my car.

Here's a tip: It turns out if you park in front of

a police station with a police placard on your windshield, your car is pretty safe.

But the most noticeable thing was that the fog had finally rolled in, and my T-shirt and jeans weren't enough covering to keep the shivers off. I cranked the heat up and turned off of Bryant onto Sixth Street, across Market onto Taylor, and then turned west onto one-way Pine Street with its timed lights that would allow me to roll fluidly out to Masonic, and from there onto Geary toward the beach and home. As I neared the ocean the fog grew heavy enough that I had to put on the windshield wipers.

When I pulled up to my house, the driveway was blocked by a dust-covered black Lexus SUV. Blocking a driveway in San Francisco is a lethal-injection offense.

I could always call and have Catherine's car towed, but there was nobody in her car. Brett or Lulu, my wager being on Lulu, had let Catherine into my house in spite of my flawed instructions to Collin.

≈37≈

I kept driving, turning left at Anza and then left again on 47th Avenue. I pulled over and got out my phone. Collin had sent me a text while I was being questioned by the detectives:

Lulu let her in w a gorilla Brown Braun Brain? B&L in LR w them. Hiding BR closet sorry & HELP! 911?

I texted back asking if the visitors were armed, and Collin replied, *IDK maybe.*

I texted that I was on the way with reinforcements and to sit tight, but then I stared at my phone, stumped for what to do next.

If I called the police, would Catherine and her son turn my family into a hostage crisis? If I went in alone, would any of us survive? So I called my personal security expert.

"Help," I said. "She's in the house with that

big gorilla from the mine. She's got Lulu and Brett. Collin's upstairs hiding, texting me. I saw her car and pulled around the block to 47th."

"Stay on the phone."

I stayed on the phone. We didn't talk while I listened to air and Thorne made his fast, silent way to where I was parked. In less than a minute he was at the passenger door and then in the car.

"Where were you, that you got here so fast?"

"Seal Rock Inn."

"Did you see her arrive at the house?"

"Yes."

"And you didn't stop her?"

"You weren't home."

I stared at Thorne, trying to fathom what he was really saying.

"But they're my family. She could *kill* them."

"She won't. They're leverage. You have the letter."

"She parked across the driveway because wants me to know she's in there with them."

He nodded.

"But still..." I said.

"You wanted to do this yourself," Thorne said.

I thought back to three nights ago, to our stay at the Seal Rock Inn while my house was commandeered by the cops. I remembered struggling to understand how so much preposterous chaos could have upended my orderly life, and my conclusion that restoring or establishing the order and control implied by the Emperor Card had to be up to me.

"Well that's true, I did say that," I said. "But that was before. In this situation I need some eloquent action, and in that department you're the most eloquent fellow I know."

He smiled that infinitesimal corner-lifting smile of his, and we climbed out of the car to go rescue my brothers and sister and pets. I took my keyring but left my purse with Dad's letter and will locked in the car trunk. If Catherine wanted the paperwork she'd have to trade some all-in-one-piece siblings for it, and once the siblings were safe Thorne would make her and her portly flunky of a son sorry they'd blocked my driveway, much less held my family captive.

"Wait," Thorne said, and it occurred to me at the same time that we didn't have to sneak into the house and maybe face gunfire.

It's always smarter to avoid a fight than to try to win one.

"Parking and Traffic," I said, naming the most fearsome civic entity in the City by the Bay.

We went back to the car and I made the call. Then I texted Collin that the cavalry was on its way and I drove around the block, parking a dozen yards up the street from my driveway. After midnight on this particular slow weeknight the tow truck and police cruiser showed up within half an hour. I showed my driver's license to prove it was indeed my residence they were tow-ing some numbskull away from. I pointed at my car, unable to enter my garage, and I made the Exasperated Resident face.

Tow trucks make noise doing their jobs. Gumball lights flash, winches creak, radios squawk. Lights went on in neighboring houses.

Thorne disappeared into the trees in Sutro Park while I dealt with the ticketing officers and the tow truck operator. I stood under the overhang of the bay window above the garage door, out of the heavy mist. Also out of any sightline from the house.

I made sure the tall African-American officer, Kelvin being the name on his badge, stood with me chatting. Officer Kelvin looked like he worked out a lot, and while we chatted I picked up that he had a functioning brain installed. I was going to have to rely on that.

The front door of my house opened and Catherine stalked outside, already shouting at the tow truck driver to stop. He'd heard that sort of thing before, and he made no move to suspend what he was doing. The SUV's front end rose steadily upward until it was high enough off the ground to haul away.

When Catherine saw me and realized I had her in check, she opted to play nice.

"Alexandra, sweetheart, why are you doing this to me?"

"Because you're holding my family hostage, and you've made it a matter for the police."

I turned to Officer Kelvin and asked him if he would mind keeping Catherine restrained while he either accompanied me upstairs to eject Allan, or called for backup because Allan might be armed, or got Catherine to summon Allan outside so I could get the two of them out of my house.

Officer Kelvin's right hand shifted to the top of his holster.

I give Catherine credit for persistence. She did her best to convince the cop that she was my stepmother, that it was my stepbrother inside with my other siblings and nothing to concern the forces of law and order about, that it was just a family disagreement and there was no need for all this fuss, and that I was being extremely unreasonable.

I disagreed, suggested Officer Kelvin put her in the back seat of his cruiser for safekeeping and contact Walt Giapetta if he had any questions about why taking Catherine into custody might be advisable. I reminded him about the murder that had taken place just a few days ago in my back yard, mentioned that Allan and Catherine might both have been responsible for it, asserted that it was an unproven claim that she was a relative, and finished by saying that no matter what he decided to do I wanted both of these people out of my home now please.

Perhaps it was the magic word that did the trick. Officer Kelvin hailed his partner, took Catherine by the arm, handed her off still protesting to his stern-looking partner, and clicked on his shoulder radio. I heard him talking to Dispatch but before he could be connected to Walt, Thorne opened the front door of my house and sent Allan sprawling out onto the sidewalk. Thorne nodded to me and stepped backward, shutting the door and locking Allan out.

"Run!" Catherine yelled at Allan. She yanked without success at the hold the officer had on her arm.

Allan picked himself up and began to lumber away toward Anza Street. Officer Kelvin, without letting go of the buttons on his radio mic, caught up with Catherine's obedient but out-of-shape son in three strides and had him down on the ground with his hands behind his back.

Brett, Collin, Lulu, and I were questioned in the living room, one by one. Leaning against the wall of the living room before the evidence technicians gathered it up was an unloaded shotgun, the removed shells sitting on the entry table. By the time all the statements had been taken and Catherine and Allan were formally arrested for home invasion and carted away, it was almost dawn.

Walt Giapetta took over investigating whether either or both Catherine and Allan had stabbed my father and dumped him into my garden. My vote was that it took both of them to do the awful job, and they were so arrogant that there was bound to be evidence: fingerprints, shoeprints,

DNA, bloodstains.

Thorne had cleared out as soon as he'd disarmed and ejected Allan. He was probably sleeping peacefully in his hotel room up at the corner.

Lulu, horrified that she'd let the two villains into the house, slunk into the kitchen when released from the interviewing and evidence-gathering action taking place in the living room. She baked dozens of oatmeal raisin cookies and handed them out to all the law enforcement personnel, and then to her family. They hit the spot.

This time, I'm guessing because nobody was killed or injured, the police allowed us to stay in the house.

"Thank God you finally got here," Collin said. "I really had to pee. It was like the worst game of Hide and Seek ever."

≈38≈

Collin found the bill of lading using the numbers I'd given him. Dad had used his real name as the shipper, I suppose to make it easier for a family member to step in "if something went wrong," which I guess is the category murder falls into.

The ship bringing the forty-foot prepaid containers to the U.S. had sailed from China and docked first in Los Angeles before sailing on to Oakland. The containers had originally traveled from the Philippines to China on a small chartered freighter plying the waters of eastern Asia. Once at the transpacific port of Ningbo the containers had been transferred onto a huge cargo ship for the thirty-five-day cruise halfway across the world.

The two containers, carrying "hand-made pottery," cleared through Customs without a hitch after being offloaded in Oakland. They were now waiting to be transported elsewhere by rail or truck. Armed with a death certificate and a notarized document establishing me as executor of Dad's estate, I could arrange to transport the containers anywhere I liked, in the meantime paying storage while the containers sat stacked atop each other at the immense East Bay facility.

"How did you know what the bill of lading number was?" Collin asked me after we'd all slept away most of the day following Catherine's arrest.

"Look at it," I said, pointing at the printout he'd given me. See anything familiar about those numbers?"

"Well damn," he said, pointing as well. "The first six are your date of birth and the second six are Dad's. How did you know?"

"Can you wait until we're all together? It's a long story."

So we gathered at Nora's house for dinner with all the children there to cheer us up. Thorne joined us for the meal, and the kids remembered him from when he'd been their deceased mother's bodyguard. They seemed to like him, or maybe they were just fascinated by the size and stillness of him, as were most of the adults if their stares were any indication.

The littlest children, once excused from the table, dragged him into the game room and proceeded to crawl around on him, giggling madly.

He allowed them to pretend they could pin him to the carpet, Gulliver and the Lilliputians. Now and then I heard him growl, and the kids screamed happily.

After the children had burned off the last of their day's energy and were sent to bath and bedtime, Thorne took a chair against the dining room wall, out of the discussion. The family sat around the table with mugs of coffee and tea and glasses of water, ready to hear what I had to tell them.

I explained things slowly, guarding my words. I remembered the Sword and Wand cards in the café Tarot reading, with their meanings of argument and disruption, and there was certainly some of that as I spoke and answered questions.

Nora's husband Hal held her hand and stayed silent. Mater kept trying to establish her right to be included in all decisions, and Brett, bless him, kept reminding her that she was included in the get-together as a courtesy, not a requirement.

There was a lot to decide, and there were five of us trying to agree on any given decision. Dad's will gave me absolute authority, but I hesitated to assert it. I finally suggested a ground rule: If we didn't all agree, I would do nothing until we did. That seemed to settle folks down.

Right away we had to grapple with the reality of Dad's doing something highly illegal. Between the faked death, the assumed identity, the possible recovery of stolen war loot, the probable falsified shipping information and gold smuggling, and his undoubted intention to circumvent tax laws, there was a lot to consider. We had to accept that our father had become what he always loathed: a crook.

But people do alter in major ways when circumstances drive them to it. Addiction, loss, shunning by his family and friends—all could have driven my father to actions he never would have engaged in previously. The four-square foundation the Emperor sits on had shattered for my Dad, and he went about establishing a new realm for himself that was the opposite of the one he'd commanded before.

And yet he'd seen it as making amends, based on what he wrote in his letter to me. He'd justified everything by saying it was all done to make up for letting his wife and children suffer when he was a drunk and unable to be a "good" father.

The upshot was that the five of us couldn't agree on what to do, so we agreed to do nothing until a decision was forced on us. The room went quiet once we agreed to leave things alone for now and just get through Dad's second funeral.

Chastened by the sense of failure I felt, I drove my siblings back to my house and left them there. They were propping armchairs under the bolted front and back doorknobs as I left.

I walked up the street past the deserted park to join Thorne at the Seal Rock Inn.

≈34≈

Three days later Catherine and Allan, who'd left fingerprints on the knife and footprints and DNA by the garden fence, were charged with murder. The police investigation found that the marriage she'd claimed was another fraud. Olivia Marcotte confirmed by phone what I'd told Walt Giapetta, and she was already booked for a new mine consulting gig in Canada.

Dad's remains were released to the crematory I chose. We paid for an obituary to appear in the *Chronicle* and chartered a yacht so we could scatter his ashes at sea, as we had done for Harry Lamirato years before. Collin and Lulu and Nora took turns pouring out the lumpy gray contents of the crematorium box. Brett read Tennyson's "Crossing the Bar," and I read Jane Kenyon's "Let Evening Come." The five of us then stood in a circle, held hands, and Collin said a prayer thanking

God that we had each other, and that we'd been born Josiah Bard's children.

That night we held a wake for friends and family at my house rather than at Nora and Hal's. Their kids would have been kids, none of whom had ever met their grandfather Josiah, and so the consensus was that this particular wake should be for adults. I hired a caterer for the care and feeding of one and all. The house was crowded with friends from when my siblings and I were all still living in San Francisco.

Mater's chums Charlotte and Ann and DeDe came to provide support for the "widow," and with them came Charlotte's husband and Ann's as well. They took over the living room couch and side chairs and were talking quietly and catching the caterer's eye on a regular basis to make sure their wine glasses were topped up with chardonnay and pinot grigio.

DeLeon, his wife Maxine, and their three grown offspring arrived with hugs and a little bouquet of white roses.

There was a collective gasp from Mater's contingent when Bix Bonebreak appeared by himself at the top of the stairs in the front hallway.

"I hope your wife is doing well," I said, going to him and taking his sandpapery hand in both of mine. He shook his head. I tried to lead him to the kitchen, but he'd seen DeDe and she'd seen him.

She stood and stepped over the outstretched legs that Mater refused to fold up so DeDe could step easily past the coffee table. I backed away from Bix so DeDe could take both his hands in hers and tell him how glad she was to see him after all these years, and how sorry she was to hear about his wife's illness. She told him she'd lost her husband to cancer, so she could maybe understand a little of what he and his kids must be going through, and oh heavens this was a wake for Josh so she'd go back to where she'd been sitting and mind her own business. She just wanted him to know that he and his wife and family continued to be in her thoughts and prayers.

DeDe said all that while tears streaked down her cheeks unchecked.

Then Jeremy McDunnigan arrived.

≈40≈

"I came to pay my respects," Jeremy said.

"No, you didn't," I said, and then Thorne was standing next to me, looking like he was ready to toss Jeremy backwards down the stairs.

Jeremy held up his hands, palms out, in a "hold on" gesture, and said, "You're right. I'm sorry."

I studied him, and then Thorne reached and pulled open Jeremy's black cashmere sport coat on each side, looking for a weapon.

"Turn," Thorne said, and Jeremy turned to let Thorne lift up the back of the jacket and inspect the waistband of his slacks.

"Lift your pant legs" was the next command, and Jeremy complied, as everyone does when Thorne issues an order.

I flagged Brett, who was talking to DeLeon in the dining room, and told him I was going to take

Jeremy downstairs to Thorne's apartment.

Once there, Thorne and I sat flanking Jeremy. I wasn't wearing the magic red jacket, but he started talking as soon as we were in our chairs.

"I know you have the containers. I want to make a deal with you."

"What containers?" I said.

"Oh cut the crap, Xana. Catherine told me about the letter, so it's clear that your Dad communicated something to you before he died. It had to be the shipment information."

"Not before he died. Before your sister killed him."

He cleared his throat. "All right."

"Why should I do anything for you?" I said.

"Because what are you going to do with the containers? You'd have to arrange for intermodal transfer and storage. You don't know how to handle the contents once you get the containers somewhere where you can process them."

"But you know what to do."

"Yes."

"The bill of lading says they contain pottery."

"You and I both know that's not all they contain. Your father used the money we gave him to single-handedly bring out the gold and valuables from the caves. He bought two pack animals and dug it all out by hand and carried it down to a town on Luzon. He built a little foundry and taught himself how to melt the gold down into ingots. He hired local potters to make lidded jars so the shipment's weight wouldn't be suspicious. When the potters went home in the evening he placed the cooled ingots in the kiln-baked pots, covered the ingots with a lot of raffia, and taped the lids on. The pots went onto shipping pallets, and the pallets went into the containers, and when everything was loaded up he shipped it back to the States. You've got the containers, but you don't know what to do with them."

"What are you offering?"

"I'm offering to take them off your hands."

"In exchange for?"

"In exchange for not alerting the authorities to the smuggling of contraband into the country."

"Oh, Jeremy, I don't think that's the deal at all. You want what's in those pots so much that you and your sister and nephew were willing to kill my father for it. You won't alert anybody if it means you'll lose what's in that shipment."

Jeremy sat back and studied me the way a watchdog tilts his head to study a potential burglar. To bite or not to bite?

"Well, then, perhaps we can agree on terms," he said.

"Perhaps."

"What did you have in mind?"

"Nope. You want the containers, you make me an offer for them."

"They're not doing you any good sitting there, and you don't have the resources to handle them."

"They're not doing you any good either, and I can afford to let them sit there forever. Or I can sell them to someone else and let the buyer find out what's in the pots. Tell me how you plan to handle them."

He thought, his fingers pulling at his chin, and finally said, "I'm going to truck them up to the mine."

"Meaning you still plan to go through with falsifying the assays and bilking your investors."

"No. That plan is dead now that my sister and nephew are in jail. But I own the mine, and it's on six hundred acres with a locking gate. Mariposa is an out-of-the-way location where I can take my time opening the jars and retrieving the gold in small quantities. That way I can unload it without creating a stir, and I can work without people looking over my shoulder wondering what I'm up to. Hell, I can even keep the pottery business going in order to mask the whole effort."

I looked at Thorne. He raised his eyebrows a micrometer to let me know he agreed with allowing this guy to try to pull off his plan. Let Jeremy get stuck with the illegal goods, since my siblings and I couldn't easily do anything with them now that we had them.

"Make me an offer," I repeated.

"Five hundred thousand. That's easy to divide between the five of you."

"Jeremy, I've changed my mind. Get out of my house, please. Right now. Your sister, probably with your collusion, killed my father, and I don't want your money. The containers can sit and rust."

"No! I didn't know my sister would kill Josh. How would I get the information we needed if Josh was dead? Catherine has a bad temper. I'm very sorry about Josh."

I stood up because I was afraid I was going to hit him, very hard, someplace that would hurt him very much. He stood up and stepped backward, holding up his hands.

"Please wait. At least talk it over with your family. I'll up the offer. This is just a negotiation now. Get your family involved before you rule out a deal."

"I'm the sole executor, so my decision is the only one that counts."

"I respect that. I'm just suggesting how you might proceed. Josh did a lot of work, went to a lot of lengths to get the gold back here. I know he did that for you guys. At least take into account that he'd want his children to have some benefit from all his sacrifices."

"I'll think about it and let you know," I said, pointing at the door.

He edged around me. "I'll call tomorrow, after you've had a chance to discuss it with your family."

After we heard the front door close behind Jeremy Thorne hugged me, pulling me close and kissing the top of my head.

"Brett," he said.

"Of course."

Brett is the family arch-negotiator. Time to put him to work negotiating a price for a commodity slightly more valuable than frozen pork bellies.

≈41≈

After the last of the wake attendees left, I asked Nora to stay and told my siblings about Jeremy's attempt to buy the containers, and Thorne's suggestion that Brett do the negotiating. As usually happens when the right idea is suggested, everyone immediately agreed that it was the way to go.

Over the next two days, my eldest brother did a superb job of wringing every possible cent out of Jeremy. Brett sat punching calculator buttons, factoring in container and pallet and clay weight against the weight of gold per ounce, and came up with a plausible estimate as to how much gold was actually in the containers. He and Jeremy video-conferenced for hours on their PCs, churning out numbers and finally coming to terms.

Based on the estimated volume of gold and the current price per ounce on the gold market,

Brett got Jeremy to waive repayment of all the prior funds invested in the Philippines project so that he couldn't come back later and claim that Dad's estate owed him anything. Jeremy took full title on the foundry and pottery Dad had set up.

In addition, Brett got Jeremy to pay out twenty million in cash to the estate, so that I could submit the handwritten will into probate and pay the proper taxes.

Brett then handled the container consignment and, once the funds transfer from Jeremy to the estate's bank account was completed, I handed over the signed-off paperwork. Jeremy finally owned what he had paid so much for over the years.

It was done.

≈42≈

Collin, hugging me and kissing my cheek as he and Brett and Lulu left to go back to their own homes, said, "About that Thorne fellow..." and I smiled.

"Xana, my darling little sister, he is totally awesome in every way, and I am so happy for you. I wish you could have seen him appear out of nowhere and just take the shotgun away from that guy and hand it to Brett, and then pick that asshole up and carry him downstairs by his belt and collar and toss him out like the trash he was. Meanwhile, I have every confidence you are complying with the most important WASP commandment."

"Remind me."

"Thou Shalt Have Sex But Thou Shalt Not Enjoy It."

"Uh oh," I said.

≈43≈

Three weeks later, as Thorne and I sat bundled up on the deck enjoying the afternoon fog and the unending susurration of the Pacific beyond the Sutro cliffs, the house phone rang. I had been close to nodding off from lack of sleep.

Lying awake night after night, I had tried unsuccessfully to reconcile my new father with the old one, and I nearly ignored the ringing. But there had been calls from family members since Dad's ash-scattering, so I got up to answer the phone.

"You fucking bitch!" a man shrieked.

I said "No," and hung up.

The phone rang again. This time I looked at Caller ID and saw "Franciscan Frères" so I answered, and it was Jeremy. If steam could have come out of the earpiece it would have.

"It's all fucking pottery," he said.

It took a moment for me to grasp what he was actually angry about.

"Well, that's what the bill of lading said it was."

"You know very well that that's not what I bought for *twenty million dollars*."

"Jeremy, we sold you the containers and their contents plus foundry and pottery businesses in the Philippines. What you agreed to pay for those is simply the result of a capable negotiation by my brother."

"You don't understand. We had to construct a new identity for Josh so he could disappear and reappear as a new person, because bankers in the Philippines knew Josiah. He'd been the bank's representative, financing nickel mining over there before they shut most of the mines down over some environmental bullshit. The local mine owners would have gotten wind that Josh was there and they'd have gone after him, just because they wanted an American scapegoat.

"We had no problem faking a death and creating a new identity," he went on.. "But you and I both know he went over there as somebody else because he was supposed to retrieve gold, not a bunch of pots. He *told* us he found it and was bringing it back. I've been through every single pallet and every single pot. There's not one ounce of gold in the lot."

"So you're saying Dad started a business, actually two businesses if you include the foundry, and employed how many people?"

"Over a hundred."

"Were they all former nickel miners, by any chance?"

"What difference does that make?" he yelled.

"I thought so," I said. "Well, apparently it made a difference to my father that he could try to make amends with some of the people who were put out of work, even if he wasn't the reason they became unemployed."

"I don't give a *shit* about your father making amends. You and your shark of a brother cheated me, and you owe me twenty million dollars, plus interest, plus the initial investment we made setting your father up, paying off the family of the guy whose name Josh took, and setting up these ridiculous businesses."

Jeremy took a breath and blew it out.

"He bought mules, for Chrissake. Turns out the mules were for hauling cartloads of clay deposits down to the pottery. Altogether, including the Mariposa mine and the Philippines expedition, the investment comes to thirty million plus change, but I'll round it down, just for old time's sake."

I laughed. I couldn't help myself. Jeremy tried to halt the laughter by saying "Stop!" again and again, but it had been a difficult few weeks and the grief and the nerves and the insomnia took over. For a full minute I was essentially hysterical.

I felt Thorne looming behind me, and then the heat from his big hand on my shoulder. I calmed down.

"Jeremy," I said, "Let me get this straight. You entered into an agreement with Josiah Wayfield Bard to, unbeknownst to him, defraud your mining investors, during the course of which plot you funded his fake death and assumption of a false identity. You paid for him to travel to the Philippines using that false identify so he could search for a mythical gold cache, during the course of which he was to set up, with your agreement and financial backing, two businesses, one of which produced pottery. You arranged to have the finished pottery shipped to Oakland, after which my father refused to cooperate further because he learned of your intended fraud of the Mariposa mine investors. Your sister pretended that she and my father had gotten married so that if he died she could claim the right to inherit, and then she and her son proceeded to track my father down when they heard from Pete Agostino that Dad was back with the gold. They stabbed Dad to death in my back yard so Catherine could steal the paperwork on the shipped containers. When she didn't find the papers on my Dad, she and your nephew held my family hostage in order to extort the papers from me. Oh, and they blocked my driveway while they were at it. How'm I doin' so far?"

"Xana, you know none of that is the point."

"Jeremy, all of that is precisely the point, so here's what you can do. Take a look at your documents. Nothing on anything you have in your possession says anything about gold. If it did, it would be illegal to have brought it into the U.S. You bought finished pottery and a pottery-making enterprise. If you paid too high a price for it, that's just a poor business negotiation on your part."

"Somebody has that gold. It has to be you. You'll be hearing from my lawyers."

"I think not. Mostly because I don't have any gold, because the gold is a myth. So if your lawyers are ethical they'll tell you you're nuts, and also too stupid to be trusted with a pen and a checkbook. If they're unethical, they'll lie to you and soak you for some more money that won't be spent to any purpose."

Jeremy raised his voice again. I held the phone away from my ear. He was yelling that the mine debacle on top of a thirty-million-dollar unrecoverable loss were going to be enough to lose him his partnership.

I hung up. I started to laugh again but Thorne pulled me into his arms. I smelled cotton shirt and vetiver soap, and that was all it took for me to settle.

≈44≈

Thorne and I went back out to the deck, but instead of sitting in my chair I sat on his lap and he held me while I told him about the empty pots.

"How are you?" he said when I finished.

"I think I can sleep now."

He patted my hip, where his hand was resting.

"I couldn't reconcile the father I knew with the person he seemed to have become. Fathers and daughters, it's a heavy-duty relationship. I built my own character on the foundation of my Dad's integrity. To have this preposterous chaos erupt around Dad in a way that seemed to characterize him as the thing he hated most made me rethink everything I used to be able to trust without question."

Thorne hummed, encouraging me to talk

through where I was with everything that had happened.

"Trust is what it's all built on, isn't it?" I said.

"The only solid ground there is."

"The Emperor Card, with the foundation his throne sits on that makes his realm possible, is about rock-solid trust. My Dad was willing to pursue the lost gold as long as it was a straight deal: Find it and, since there's no way to make reparation at this point or find the original owners, make what good use of it you can. Put some poor people to work and take care of your family. But when he found out Jeremy was going to cheat people with his share, Dad refused. I see my father again in that move. It cost him his life, but I think he accepted the risk. If my Dad gave you his word, keeping his word was worth his life to him."

"Old school," Thorne said.

"Shouldn't be. It should be a perennial. Would you be with me if I weren't like my Dad in that way?"

I looked up at him, at the dark green eyes with the yellow flecks. He met my gaze and shook his head no.

"You don't need the red jacket," he said. I looked a question up at him.

"People know the truth. They know honesty when they encounter it. You sit and ask questions and genuinely listen. You allow people to tell you what they want to tell you, and they feel heard.

Most of the time people match honesty with honesty. People tend to trade a lie for a lie and a truth for a truth."

"Whew, Thorne. Biblical."

He smiled his barely discernible smile. I settled back against him and we sat, surrounded by the white noises of the ocean and the windblown leaves of the Sutro Park eucalyptus trees, until the doorbell rang.

Because of Jeremy's phone call, Thorne went to answer the door. I stood to one side at the top of the stairs, behind the living room wall.

Thorne opened the door after seeing Bix Bonebreak's face through the beveled glass. Next to Bix were two rolling Pullman-size suitcases, hard-sided gray plastic with extended handles.

"Hi Bix. Moving in?" I said.

"It's been a month," he said. "The note said to wait a month and then bring these to you."

I invited him in. He hefted one suitcase inside and up the stairs. Bix is a big strong man, but I could see from the strain on his face that lifting the suitcase inside the door took effort, and that he was glad to set it down on the entryway hardwood. Thorne saw that too, and stepped out to hoist the second suitcase inside the house. He made a sound when he lifted it, so it must have weighed a great deal indeed. After hauling the big bags up the stairs, both men looked relieved to set the cases down and roll them from the top of the stairs into the kitchen.

"Can I get you anything? Coffee, some iced tea or water?" I asked Bix.

He asked for ice water, and he held his silence until we were all seated with refreshments.

"How is Bonnie?" I said, naming his wife.

"She's gone. Last week," he said.

"I'm so sorry. I hadn't heard."

"She didn't want an obituary or a service."

"Is there a charity she cared about?"

Bix waved the question off.

"She was very private. You don't have to do anything. I know you never met her, but she was a good woman, and she was good to me. She was a wonderful mother to our kids."

I put my hand on his and nodded. We sat for a moment. Bix looked out the window at the park next door and then turned to me. He pulled a folded envelope from his pocket and handed it to me.

"Four suitcases came by courier right after you left my office last month."

I opened the envelope and read Dad's handwriting. I put the note down on the counter because I couldn't read it with my hands shaking.

> *Bix, if I don't come and claim these I*
> *want you to hold onto the cases for a month*
> *and then deliver the gray ones to my*
> *daughter Alexandra. Hand deliver them to*
> *her only and no one else. If a woman named*
> *Catherine Wolf says she's my wife and you*
> *should give her the cases, she's lying.*

I'm headed to Alexandra's to tell her what's going on, but I'm planning for contingencies. I'm concerned that crooks are going to cause trouble for a while, and I don't want Xana to know about these cases until things have settled down.

The black cases go to Pete Agostino in Winnemucca. I'm pretty sure Xana will know how to find him if you can't.

I've enclosed repayment of your life-saving loan. Your friendship has been a treasure to me.

Josh

"There were fifty hundreds in that envelope," Bix said.

"The money you gave him the night he disappeared."

Bix nodded.

"Then what's in the suitcases?"

"I don't know. I just know the cases are all as heavy as a box of rocks. I sent the other ones off to Winnemucca this morning."

Bix looked up at the kitchen clock, checking the time.

"Pete Agostino should have his by now," he said.

"Well, let's take a look then, shall we?"

"I don't have to see what's in them," Bix said, standing up to go. "I think maybe they're just between you and Josh."

"Please," I said. "I'd like you to know. You

were Dad's best—maybe his only—friend. He trusted you, and he was right to."

I moved the drink glasses out of the way. The two men heaved one suitcase up onto the island and I flipped open the metal clasps. Inside were thirty-five or forty large padded envelopes. We pulled them out, put the empty suitcase down on the floor, and read the envelopes' labels: Em, Di, Ru, Sa, Sph, Pe, Aq, Sp, Ja. I slit open the one labeled "Em" and out tumbled hundreds of faceted green gems.

"Oh my God, they can't be emeralds."

But they were. The other envelopes contained diamonds, rubies, sapphires, sphenes, peridots, aquamarines, spinels, and jade.

I bent down to open the second case on the floor. Inside were fifty or sixty padded envelopes, each labeled AU.

I brought a surprisingly heavy one up to the counter and opened it. Out slid dozens of gleaming wafers, the color of the metal unmistakable. They were stamped "24K" and "500g," and in a cartouche in the center of each was stamped an image of Shakespeare.

Thorne pointed at the cartouche.

"Bill," he said.

"Well, damn," said Bix. "The fucking Bard."

We were speechless for a few minutes, picking up and putting down jewels and mini-ingots.

I looked at Thorne and then at Bix.

"I can be my father's daughter again."

Emotion caught in my throat and blurred my vision.

Bix grinned, showing big white Chiclets-sized teeth. I walked around the island to hug him. Thorne reached out to shake Bix's hand, and both big men laughed—Thorne in a deep, rhythmic rumble and Bix with his sharp bark.

Turning back, I cleared my throat and used my forearm to sweep the treasure to one side. I pulled open the diamond envelope, pouring out the flashing jewels onto the countertop.

White, black, chocolate, pink, green, yellow, orange, champagne and blue stones cut into rounds, squares, ovals, pears, and marquises scattered across the marble surface. They caught the light and refracted blinding, brilliant prismatic color.

"Choose one," I said to Bix. "A big one. For DeDe."

Bevan Atkinson, author of *The Tarot Mysteries* including *The Fool Card, The Magician Card, The High Priestess Card,* and *The Empress Card,* lives in the San Francisco Bay Area and is a long-time tarot card reader.

Bevan currently has no pets but will always miss Sweetface, the best, smartest, funniest dog who ever lived, although not everyone agrees with Bevan about that.

CPSIA information can be obtained
at www.ICGtesting.com
Printed in the USA
FFOW02n0436260617
37148FF

9 780996 942553